This weekend wa
and-dried as she' ... **pecially**
when her whole body tingled and her
breath caught each time she locked eyes
with the man.

Yes, they were supposed to act like a couple for the next three days, but it was supposed to be pretend.

Except this connection between them felt all too real.

If the plane hadn't bumped them around earlier, she would've kissed him again.

Would've done a lot more, too, if they'd been alone. She wanted him. Intensely.

Like she'd never wanted anything ever.

Which made no sense, and Carmen was a sensible person. She didn't go around acting on her impulses, didn't throw caution to the wind. She was the stable one, the caregiver, the person other people depended on. No matter how gorgeous he was or how he made want throb through her like molten lava, she could not let him overwhelm her good sense. She'd lived her whole life putting others before herself, always putting their needs before her own, always biding her time.

She'd just have to suffer through the temptation as well as she could and make the best of it.

Dear Reader,

This is the third and final book set within my Anchorage Mercy world. These characters feel like family now, including Zac and Carmen. EMT Zac played a minor role in my first two books, but he was begging for his own story and finally it's here! He's the best paramedic in Anchorage, but his personal life is a mess—mainly due to family drama and trust issues stemming from his relationship with his father.

Carmen Sanchez, the hardworking midwife from my second book, is the perfect heroine for Zac. She's up for a big promotion at a new clinic in California and plans to have her final interview with her potential new bosses at the national midwife convention. Only trouble is, she may have told her family-oriented new employer she was engaged in order to get the job. Now she's in need of a fake fiancé pronto, so she turns to her old friend and former flame, Zac.

Plenty of trouble and sexy shenanigans ensue over a weekend of pretend romance. But can Zac and Carmen put the past to rest and reach their true happily-ever-after?

Read *A Weekend with Her Fake Fiancé* to find out!

Traci

A WEEKEND WITH HER FAKE FIANCÉ

TRACI DOUGLASS

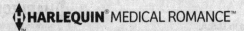

Recycling programs
for this product may
not exist in your area.

ISBN-13: 978-1-335-14918-3

A Weekend with Her Fake Fiancé

First North American Publication 2019

Copyright © 2019 by Traci Douglass

Printed in U.S.A.

Books by Traci Douglass

Harlequin Medical Romance

One Night with the Army Doc
Finding Her Forever Family
A Mistletoe Kiss for the Single Dad

Visit the Author Profile page at Harlequin.com.

CHAPTER ONE

CERTIFIED NURSE-MIDWIFE Carmen Sanchez
swiped the back of her wrist across her forehead, careful to avoid the blood staining her
glove. "One more strong push and the baby will
be out." She gave Teena, her twenty-eight-year-
old patient, an encouraging smile. "You can do
it."

"I can't!" Teena panted, her head lolling to
one side on the pillows. "I'm too tired."

Fifteen hours of labor would do that to a person, but there was only one way out of this and
it was through. Having Teena's husband there
for moral support would have been ideal, but the
poor man was working on a fishing boat somewhere in the Bering Sea right now and couldn't
be reached.

"I know you're exhausted, Teena," she said,
her Caribbean accent drawing out the name.
"But you've done such a wonderful job so far.
All you need is the strength to push one more

time on your next contraction and you'll have your son in your arms. Don't you finally want to hold him? After all these long months? Think of your husband's face when he sees his son."

Teena bit back a sob and nodded.

"Right." Carmen used her most authoritative voice. "Then push as hard as you can when I tell you, okay?"

The patient nodded and took a deep breath.

It was Teena's first pregnancy, and she'd been a difficult case from the outset, with sickle cell anemia complicating matters. Carmen had worked in conjunction with an obstetrician and a hematologist to monitor the patient and provide a safe delivery.

Another contraction hit and time seemed to slow as Teena groaned.

"Go!" Carmen got into position. "That's it. Good. *Good.* Push!"

Teena leaned up on her elbows and bore down hard, toes curled and muscles straining. Finally the baby's head crowned, followed in short order by one shoulder, then two. At last the tiny infant slipped into Carmen's waiting hands and her patient flopped back onto the bed, exhausted.

Carmen cut the umbilical cord, then handed the baby to a waiting nurse, who wrapped the new arrival in a blanket and suctioned its tiny mouth and nose. Soon the boy's wailing filled the room and Teena cried again, this time with relief and joy.

Once the afterbirth was dealt with, Carmen took a moment to enjoy the wonder. Even after years in practice the addition of a new life into the world still amazed her.

She slipped out into the hall, walking over to the desk at the nurses' station so she could decompress and document the backlog of charts awaiting her.

Before she'd finished with the first one, she was interrupted.

"Just the woman I was looking for."

Carmen's heart tripped at the deep male voice, and she glanced up to see Zac Taylor. The zing of attraction she felt was decidedly inconvenient, given he was a paramedic and they saw each other a lot, both in the course of their work and hanging out with mutual friends. Also, they'd spent a steamy night together a few months back, after copious amounts of alcohol at the Anchorage Mercy Hospital holiday staff party, and since then things had been a bit awkward.

Flings weren't her usual MO. Actually, love— the romantic kind—wasn't even on her itinerary, so the way her heart continued to flutter whenever he was around, despite her wishes, was beyond annoying.

It wasn't that she was against hearts and fluff. It was just that she didn't have time for such nonsense. Not with her mother to care for, in the early stages of dementia. Some days her mother was fine, other days she didn't recognize her own family. It was heartbreaking, the slow loss of the person who'd been the one constant in her life. Plus, Carmen was saving to put her younger sister through nursing school at the University of Alaska this fall, after she graduated high school. Between her own busy work schedule and her responsibilities at home Carmen was lucky to have time enough to eat and sleep, let alone date.

In fact, given her past, it was probably better for her to stay alone anyway. Growing up with virtually nothing in the poorest part of Port of Spain, Trinidad, had taught her self-reliance and self-sacrifice. There had only been so much to go around, and you'd had to look after what you got.

Carmen considered herself a tough, responsible, independent woman. Prudent. She didn't need a man to make her life happy. And if she was lonely sometimes—well, that was the price she paid for safety and security. Lord knew she couldn't rely on anyone else to give her anything.

Only problem was, she needed a favor. From Zac.

She bit her lip and watched him through her lashes as she finished her documentation.

The guy was temptation on legs. Gorgeous and charming. And the very things that drove her nuts about him were the very reasons he was the perfect choice for her needs. He had a reputation as a player. Which meant he was not a man for long-term, serious relationships. But he sure fit the bill for Mr. Fix-It-Right-Now.

"Hey, Zac," said Priya Shaw, coming out of another delivery room down the hall, and Carmen tensed.

Priya was a fellow midwife and friend. She also happened to be Carmen's biggest rival for the supervisor position at a new state-of-the-art birthing clinic in California. The job paid twice what her current salary was here at Anchorage Mercy, and the extra funds would go a long way toward getting her ailing mother into an assisted-care facility for dementia patients and also help offset the tuition fees for her sister's university education.

"Hey, P," said Zac, but his focus remained on Carmen.

He leaned an elbow on the counter beside her

and his scent—soap and fabric softener mixed with warm, clean male—wrapped around her, teasing her senses and making her far more aware of the man than she liked.

"Tell Lance I'll call him later about this weekend," Zac said to Priya.

"Will do," she called back, tucking her long dark hair behind her ear as she picked up a chart and headed into a delivery room.

Priya was engaged to Zac's best friend, local firefighter Lance Marranto—a fact that only made the favor Carmen needed more complicated. But she'd find a way to deal with it because she was a survivor.

First, though, she needed to finish this chart.

Carmen sighed and blinked down at her writing. Her normally crisp cursive was going a bit wonky from fatigue. Teena's long delivery had burned through what little energy she'd had left, considering she'd already been up late with her mother before coming in for the delivery.

Mama's memory had begun deteriorating faster recently, and the poor thing had a hard time remembering she was in Alaska now, and not back home on her warm tropical island. The night before last she'd wanted to go outside in her nightgown and walk along the beach, meaning Carmen had been up constantly to stop her. It was only early spring, and the wilds on the outskirts of Anchorage were hardly a place for a sixty-five-year-old woman to traipse around in the middle of the night.

Thankfully, Carmen's shift was almost done now. All she wanted to do was hand over Teena's care to the nurses on duty and go home for a shower and a long nap. Clara was on Mamawatch duty until tomorrow.

She yawned before she could stop herself.

"Long day?" Zac asked.

His stupid dimples were making him look far too adorable. Not that she noticed. Nope. Not at all.

"Long night too. Fifteen-hour labor." Carmen stretched her arms above her head. "Patient finally delivered this morning." She shuffled her sore feet, then closed the chart she'd completed and shoved it aside. "Why?"

"We just brought a patient into the ER and I've got a few minutes to kill. Thought maybe you'd like to grab a coffee. Looks like you need one. If you drive home now, you'll fall asleep at the wheel."

He smiled the sexy smile that always got her right in the feels. No man should be allowed to be that handsome. Seriously. The navy blue fabric of his paramedic uniform only made his dark skin glow more warmly beneath the overhead lights, and the material seemed to cling to all his rippling muscle and highlight his pure masculine grace.

"Does that kind of pick-up line work well for you?" Carmen frowned, reminding herself that Zac was off-limits, firmly in the friend zone. And that was where he needed to stay if her plan was going to work. "Telling women how awful they look?"

"C'mon," he teased. "You know you want some caffeine."

She wanted to refuse, but he was right, darn it. Plus, she needed to ask him her favor, and now seemed as good a time as any.

"Fine. One coffee. Let's go."

He chuckled. "You're cute when you're cranky."

She nudged him toward the elevator, their shoes squeaking on the shiny linoleum floor. While they waited her pulse kicked up a notch. Not because of his hotness—not entirely, anyway. No, it was nerves. She hated asking people for help. Especially when it was for a problem she'd brought upon herself.

If only she'd kept her mouth shut when the head of that clinic in California had mentioned Priya and Lance's engagement. If only she'd stopped herself from letting the easy lie roll off her tongue, sweet and potent, like the rum she'd used to serve to tourists when she'd bartended at that all-inclusive resort in Trinidad to make ends meet while paying her way through school.

Yes, I'm getting married too!

Ugh. The memory of her statement made during the interview still made her cringe.

Because she wasn't getting hitched. Hell, she hadn't even dated a man in months.

To her horror, the clinic owner had seized on that information and invited her and her non-existent fiancé to attend the upcoming national midwifery conference, where they'd announce their choice of candidate for the new job.

So here Carmen was, needing a fake fiancé for the weekend.

Unfortunately, time was running out and Carmen had only been able to come to one conclusion: Zac Taylor was the best man for the job. He was smart, funny, and not interested in forever.

Exactly what Carmen needed.

The elevator dinged and they stepped on board, the doors closing before anyone else joined them. She felt Zac's gaze on her and resisted the urge to fidget. She probably looked a mess after working all night, but it wasn't like she was trying to impress anyone—least of all him.

It wasn't as if he hadn't seen her at the end of a long shift before. They hung out together as part of a larger group of colleagues at the hospital, including doctors Jake Ryder and Molly Flynn, trauma nurse Wendy Smith and her OB doc husband Tom, plus Susan—Zac's EMT partner—and Lance and Priya, and some of the other local firefighters and their significant others. It was a large group and easygoing. Uncomplicated. The last thing she wanted to do was mess up that vibe by allowing her attraction to Zac to get any farther along than fantasy territory.

So, yeah. Zac was a friend. A friend from whom she needed a favor.

They got their drinks, then found a quiet table in the sunny atrium of the cafeteria, away from the other patrons. Sade's "Smooth Operator" was playing on the sound system overhead and Carmen couldn't contain her ironic snort. If there was a better theme song for Zac's serial dating, she didn't know it.

"What?" Zac leaned back in his chair, stretching out his long legs. He was a good foot taller than her petite five-foot-four-inch frame. "What's so funny?"

"Nothing. Just tired, I guess," she said, trying to pass off her inappropriate giggles as fatigue. "Are you off work soon too?"

"Nah. I wish… Pulling a double shift."

He sipped his iced chai tea. Zac worked almost as hard as she did, always picking up extra runs when he could. Work hard, play hard, apparently.

The favor nagged in the back of Carmen's mind, making her jittery. "Do you have plans next weekend?"

"Not sure." Zac frowned at her over the straw in his drink. "Why?"

Her cheeks flamed hotter. To distract herself, she toyed with a copper-colored curl that had escaped the ponytail at the nape of her neck. Her hair never obeyed, no matter how hard she tried to tame it into submission. She blamed her mother's Ghanaian ancestry as much as the ever-changing Alaskan weather.

"I have a thing."

"A *thing*?" Zac raised a brow at her.

"A national conference. Next weekend. I was hoping maybe you could come with me, if you're not busy."

She clutched her cup so hard the stiff cardboard threatened to collapse. She was *so* not good at this sort of thing.

Calm down. There's no reason to be nervous. This isn't a real date.

As far as their one-night stand went—well, she had no idea. But, given the fact he'd never brought it up with her, she doubted he even remembered their fling. They'd both had far too much to drink. It was water under the bridge. No reason for her pulse to race or her breath to catch. She was just another notch in his already well-scored bedpost.

An odd pain pinched her chest. Which was ridiculous. And stupid. She didn't want a relationship with Zac any more than he wanted one with her.

So why was all this causing her more stress than delivering triplets?

"Wait a minute." Zac sat forward, his dark gaze narrowed. "You're inviting me to go away with you for the weekend?"

He looked about as shocked as she felt at the proposition. Her throat tightened and she swallowed hard against the lump of unaccountable anxiety lodged there. "Yes. No. Well, not exactly." Nerves made her fumble her words. "I mean, yes. I'm inviting you to come with me for the weekend. To pretend to be my fiancé."

There. She'd done it. Asked for the favor. Now all she needed was for him to say yes.

Minutes ticked by like hours as Zac blinked at her in silence.

"Fiancé?" he said finally, his tone incredulous. "Uh… I'm going to need a few more details."

"Like what?" She frowned.

"Like *why*?"

She gave a heavy sigh and closed her eyes. "Because there's a new clinic opening in Big Sur, California, and I'm being considered for a supervisory midwife position there. If I get it, it would be a huge bump in salary. But Priya's up for the job too, and the company was really excited about her and Lance getting married. Not that being married is a requirement or anything, but I got caught up in the moment, and I didn't want to be outdone, so I told them I was getting married too."

She sighed and opened her eyes, forcing herself to keep going even as she avoided Zac's gaze.

"I realize how stupid it sounds, but the words just came out. And once I'd said them I couldn't take them back without making a fool of myself or risking being thrown out of contention for lying. So, yes. They're announcing the candidate they've chosen at the national midwifery conference and they asked me to bring along my fiancé to help me celebrate if I get the job."

She exhaled slowly and hazarded a look at Zac. He was still watching her with an unreadable expression. Her heart beat harder against her ribs as her embarrassment rose.

"If it helps, the conference is being held at a fancy resort in the Yukon called The Arctic Star. All expenses paid—even transportation. All you'd have to do is request the time off work—unless you're already scheduled to have the days free? The conference runs Thursday night through Sunday."

Zac's posture had stiffened now, she noticed, and his handsome face had gone a bit ashen. She wasn't sure if his distress had been caused by her avalanche of babbling or the fact that she'd lied to a potential employer. Both were pretty awful.

When she couldn't take the awkward silence anymore, she said, "Say something."

He shook his head and frowned. "Like what? You want me to lie for you? Pretend I'm something I'm not?"

She winced slightly at the edge in his voice. "I know this is not what you expected from me. Honestly, it's not what I expected from myself either. But now I'm stuck. Please? I never ask for favors, but I could really use your help, Zac." Feeling desperate, she added, "It's a five-star resort. They have room service, massage, a spa—the works. So you should have plenty to keep you busy while I'm in my seminars and interviews. And we'd only have to pretend to be a couple when other people are around. It's all harmless, I swear."

"Harmless? Lies are never harmless."

Zac exhaled slowly, a muscle ticking near

his tense jaw. His voice was quiet, as if he was speaking more to himself than her. She'd never seen him as anything other than a smiling charmer before, and she found the change both disconcerting and far too intriguing. She wanted to ask him why the idea bothered him so much when he was used to being with a different woman every week, but now wasn't the time.

He took a deep breath and rolled his shoulders, seeming to come to terms with something inside himself. When he met her gaze again the flash of hurt and anger she'd seen there before had been replaced by a flat guardedness.

"You're inviting me to a midwifery conference for three days at The Arctic Star Resort as your fake fiancé?"

Yep. That about summed it up.

He sat there for a moment, fiddling with his coffee cup, then finally looked up at her. "I'm not sure this is a good idea."

Crap. This wasn't going well at all. Maybe she should've waited until later, when she'd had some sleep and some time to freshen up.

Carmen did her best to keep it light, regardless of the growing heaviness in her heart. "Seriously, Zac. I know this is coming out of left field, but I wouldn't ask if I wasn't in a bind. I really need your help. It's a free weekend of luxury for you. And if you're worried I'll lose my head and seduce you, don't be. You're not my type."

"I was once."

So he *did* remember.

She opened her mouth to answer, then closed it, doing her best to hide her shock over that revelation and failing miserably. Heat prickled her cheeks and she stared at the tabletop, squeezing her cardboard coffee cup tighter than necessary.

"That night was a mistake. We were both drunk and—well, things happened. But we've moved on, right? We're friends. That's all."

He shifted and his leg brushed hers under the table. Her heart rate kicked up another notch.

"Please. It's just for three days. No commitments, no strings attached."

"Right. You keep saying that." He tapped one long, tapered finger against the side of his plastic glass. Sudden images of those fingers on her body, the way he'd touched her, stroked her, made her beg for more, flashed through her mind, unbidden.

No. No, no, no.

"Isn't there someone else you can ask? What about that guy in Radiology you were dating? Jim or John or whatever his name was?"

"Jeff." Carmen cleared her throat. "No. I can't ask him. We didn't part well. I found out he was cheating on me with his department's receptionist."

"Right." He scowled down into his tea, then sighed. "Look, it's not you. It's… Don't you have men lined up around the block wanting to go out with you?"

Flattering as his compliment was, Carmen just felt more exhausted now than she had before the coffee.

"No. There's not. Trust me. I'm not exactly a party girl around here. I work too hard. Besides, I asked you because I feel comfortable with you. We know where we stand. I won't beg, though. I'm too proud and too tired. If you say no, then I'll contact one of those online escort services to help me."

Zac gave her a look. "Arranging to spend the weekend with a guy you've never met and found on the internet? Yeah, great. Cause that's not dangerous or anything." He scrunched his nose, squinting at her. "Dammit. You really know how to put a guy on the spot, don't you? Fine. I'll go."

"Good." The relief was sudden, short-lived, as one more complication came to mind. "There is one more tiny hitch. Lance and Priya will be there too. In fact, they're flying up to the conference with us on the same private jet chartered by the Californian clinic. So we need to get our story straight ahead of time."

"Hold on. Are you nuts?" He leaned forward slightly, his voice angry. "It's bad enough we're fooling the people who might be your new bosses. Now you want me to lie to my best friend too? Because as far as Lance knows I'm not even dating anyone. I mean, we don't share all the intimate details, but he'd sure as hell have noticed if I had a fiancée sitting around somewhere."

"*Are* you dating anyone?"

"No."

"That's good, then. One less thing to worry about."

He arched a brow at her and her cheeks flushed anew.

"Darling, you've got yourself so turned around here you don't even see what you're doing."

The fact that he was probably right only served to annoy her more. "You're overthinking it. We get our stories straight, learn the basic details about each other, and keep our cool. It will be fine."

She picked at the edge of the table and kept her gaze downcast, because if she looked at him right now he'd be able to see exactly how uncomfortable she was with this, and she needed to fool him into thinking she was completely okay with it all.

She *was* completely okay with it all.

Or she would be once things got underway, because she had no choice.

"Okay. Say we do make it through this weekend. What happens if you get the job, Carmen?" Zac asked. "You get the job and you show up for work and suddenly there's no fiancé. How do you explain to the new bosses that I've disappeared from your life?"

"I'll deal with that if and when it happens."

Honestly, she didn't have the brainpower to devote to it right now. Her focus was solely on getting the job. She'd worry about the details afterward.

"We need to think of a way to get Lance and Priya to believe this has been going on for months, in secret. Maybe we could tell them we had instant chemistry and couldn't forget each other after the holiday party. That we've been seeing each other since."

Never mind that for her, at least, it was partially true. She'd never really forgotten about Zac and the way he'd made her feel that night— sexy, desired, beautiful, precious—even if it had been fueled by too much rum-spiked eggnog and fuzzy thinking.

"We need to convince them that things got serious fast and now we're ready for the next step."

Zac sat back and shook his head. "It's not going to be as easy as you think."

Carmen hid her wince—barely. "Because you're an expert in deception?"

"I've had some past experience with it, yes."

She didn't miss the flash of hurt in his dark eyes before he dropped his gaze to the floor.

"I mean, yeah, maybe your story could work. Lance has been bugging me about being off my game lately."

Her curiosity was piqued again before she could tamp it down. It was silly to think their night together had anything to do with it, but a little flare of hope still fizzed inside her anyway.

"Off your game? Since when?"

"I don't know. A couple months. I've been busy, okay? That's all." He sat forward and rubbed the spot between his brows with his fingers. "Listen, if we do this, what about all the little things couples know about each other? Birthdays, favorite colors, favorite foods, pets, personal peeves? Trust me, Lance will see right through the whole thing in two seconds flat if you don't know all that stuff about me. Hell, *he* knows all that stuff about me."

The tension inside her ratcheted higher. She'd already gotten herself neck-deep in this situation and the tide was threatening to pull her under. All she could do now was keep her head above water and roll with it.

"We'll each write it down. Create a dossier of our lives then give them to one another to memorize."

"A dossier?" Zac snorted. "What are we? Super-spies?"

"I'm serious. It's only three days. We don't need to know every detail—just the big stuff, like you said." She sighed and gave him an exasperated look. "How much of that will come up anyway? We'll be sure to avoid Lance and Priya as much as possible at the conference, just to be on the safe side. Shouldn't be hard with such a busy schedule. Okay?"

"I still think this is a mistake." After an aggrieved sigh and a flat stare, Zac said, "Okay."

Her posture sagged with relief. He wasn't making it easy, but she was glad to have it out of the way. Carmen checked her watch, then pushed to her feet and tossed her empty cup in the trash.

"Thank you. I'll text you with the flight details. And maybe you'll fill me in later about why you're so reluctant to go with me."

"Don't count on it," he said as she walked away.

Carmen glanced at him over her shoulder as she exited the cafeteria. "I never do."

Maybe you'll fill me in later about why you're so reluctant to go with me...

After Carmen had left, Zac sat alone in the cafeteria to finish his break, knowing he could never tell her the truth. His past was a secret he didn't share with anyone. For good reason.

God, he was such an idiot. He never should've accepted her offer, no matter how much he wanted to revisit the chemistry between them. There were things about him that made a return to The Arctic Star Resort reckless or insane.

Neither option made him feel better.

Never mind the fact he'd spent the last twelve years putting as much distance as possible between himself and that place. Now he was going to blow it all to smithereens in one fell swoop. All because of the chance to reconnect with the one woman he couldn't seem to forget.

Damn. The Arctic Star Resort. The conference just had to be *there*, in the one place he'd vowed never to set foot in again, owned by the one man he never wanted to lay eyes on again.

His father.

The man who'd cheated on his mother and betrayed his family's trust.

The man Zac would refuse to forgive for as long as he lived.

It was because of his father that Zac trusted no one—because of his father that he kept everyone at a distance, never letting anyone too close, never trusting anyone enough to get hurt.

It was because of him that Zac feared he was cut from the same lying, cheating cloth.

And maybe he was, considering the state of his personal life. He was a serial dater— a player, according to the local gossip mill— and he'd cultivated that reputation carefully, never letting anyone close enough to see what he feared most—that perhaps beneath the charade it was entirely too true. That perhaps he was just like his father.

He rubbed his eyes, sighing at fate, or luck, or whatever the hell had brought this mess into his life. He'd thought he'd left it all behind him for good. Started fresh, created a new future of his own making. Yet, here it was, right back on his doorstep again, and he had no one to blame but himself.

It wasn't like he could say no to Carmen. She was his friend. Never mind that he'd been secretly crushing on her since their incredible night together after that holiday party, or that what his best friend—Lance—teased him about was true. He *was* off his game. Because of her.

It didn't matter. Nothing could ever come of it.

He didn't do relationships and she was way too good for him. Had been back then—still was today.

Knowing that didn't make him want her any less, though.

Lost in thought, he didn't notice Lance walk up to his table with a half-eaten sub sandwich in one hand and a water bottle in the other until it was too late.

"Dude, shouldn't you be out cruising for trouble? You're on call today, right?"

The well-muscled firefighter plopped down uninvited in the seat across from Zac, his white T-shirt with the Anchorage Fire Department insignia embroidered on the chest pocket stretching tight over his chest, dark circles shadowing his blue eyes. All the Anchorage first responders had been pulling extra shifts lately, gearing up for tourist season in the spring.

"Your rig's still parked out in the ambulance bay."

"Susan's manning the radio. She'll text me when she needs me."

Zac stared out the window beside him, as

much to get his head together as to avoid looking at his best friend, who would too easily read that something was wrong in Zac's face. He'd never had a poker face, despite the genes he shared with his father.

He sighed and squinted at the cars coming and going outside. "Let me ask you something, Lance. Did you ever do something so dumb, so out of your comfort zone, so crazy, that you ought to have your head examined for even considering it?"

Lance snorted. "You've met Priya, right? Still can't believe she said yes when I asked her to marry me. She's way out of my league, dude."

Zac chuckled. "True. Still, things have worked out okay for you guys, right?"

"Right." Lance halted, mid-bite of his sandwich. "Wait. Are we talking about women? Because I've been wondering when you're gonna get back out there again."

Sighing, Zac scrubbed a hand over his face. He'd walked right into that, dammit. He was probably overthinking all this. Maybe Carmen was right. Maybe he should just enjoy the fact that a beautiful woman had asked him to spend the weekend with her, all expenses paid and no strings attached. Chances were his father wouldn't be at the resort anyway. He was probably off somewhere else, supervising his world-wide hotel empire. Zac hadn't kept up with the family business much since he'd left, preferring peace of mind to profit reports.

"Oh, man." Lance shoved his last bite of sandwich into his mouth, muffling his words. "The way you're all quiet, with that sad look on your face, this is definitely about a woman. Don't tell me the great Zac Taylor, player extraordinaire, has finally fallen."

Zac blinked at his good friend. No. He hadn't fallen. That was insane. Sure, he liked Carmen. And, yeah, they were friends. More than friends, if you counted that one night. But, no, he wasn't in love with her. Zac didn't *do* love. Not anymore. Keeping his boundaries intact was easier, safer. No messy emotions involved.

And if that pang of loneliness inside him nipped a bit harder when Carmen was around, well, that was just the price he paid.

This weekend wouldn't be about anything more than helping out a friend. That was all it could ever be where he was concerned.

He had too many secrets and shadows haunting him for it to be anything else.

Zac focused on the snowplow driving by, clearing the parking lot from the fresh three inches they'd just gotten.

You had to love March in Alaska.

"Well?" Lance asked, drawing Zac back to

their present conversation. "You gonna tell me her name or what?"

Zac shook his head. "There is no name because there is no mystery woman."

His friend's gaze narrowed as he zeroed in on Zac's face. "Nope. Not buying it, dude. Something's up with you, and it's not just because you haven't been playing the field lately."

"Why are you so concerned about my private life anyway, man?" Zac shrugged and gave his friend an irritated glance. "Mind your own business."

"Don't even try to change the subject." Lance grinned. "I'm right, aren't I? You *are* hung up on someone. I knew it! You've been acting differently since that holiday party. Been hanging around the apartment more…keeping to yourself."

Despite knowing this would benefit his ruse about Carmen, Zac winced internally. It rankled. Zac liked his privacy. The scandal following his father's affair had been splashed all over the tabloids, and having the spotlight glaring on him had been uncomfortable, to say the least.

It didn't help that *he'd* acted out back in the day too. He'd only been sixteen when the news had broken about his father's infidelity and he hadn't handled it well. In fact, he'd crashed the new sports car his parents had bought him and injured the girl he'd been dating at the time, who'd been his unlucky passenger. She'd made a full recovery, but Zac still lived with the guilt of his recklessness.

One more reason he'd left his parents and all their money behind. The wealth had corrupted his dad. Who was to say it wouldn't do the same to Zac?

Needing to get out of his own head and away from the pain of his past, he tried to change the subject again. "You and Priya ready for the wedding?"

Thankfully, this time Lance took the bait. "I guess… She's in charge of all that. I just show up when she tells me." He tossed his empty water bottle into the recycling bin nearby. "Like this fancy conference thing we're going to next weekend. If she gets this new job it'll mean a move to California. Not sure I'm ready to leave Alaska behind, but I guess sand and surf wouldn't be a horrible change. Plus, we could always come back to Anchorage to visit."

Zac nodded, not ready to reveal that he and Carmen would be at the conference too, and Carmen would be competing for the same position.

"Well, I don't know what you got going on behind the scenes, but I'm telling you, dude, one of these days you're going to find someone who'll knock those player socks right off you," Lance said, standing. "You'll end up in wedded bliss just like the rest of us. See you later."

Sooner than you think, buddy.

Standing too, Zac checked his watch. "I should get back to the rig. Help Susan check inventory."

"I'll walk with you." Lance followed him out of the cafeteria. "Break's over."

They rode the elevator to the first floor and headed down the hall toward the ER.

"No man is an island, remember?" Lance said, apparently not about to let the matter drop.

"Maybe I am."

Zac knew he sounded defensive—but, *damn*. Soon Lance and Priya and everyone else at that stupid conference would be all up in his business, so sue him if he wanted to fly below the radar just a little bit longer.

"Islands suit me. Some tropical place with fruity drinks and beaches for miles. I like that kind of island."

They rounded the corner into the controlled chaos of the emergency room, where people were rushing around and the air was filled with the sound of babies crying and clacking gurneys. The scent of antiseptic and lemon floor wax mingled around him like a comforting blanket.

Across the way, Zac spotted Carmen talking to Wendy Smith at the nurses' station and stopped short.

Lance glanced between Zac and Carmen and then clapped him on the shoulder and chuckled. "Sounds a whole lot like Trinidad to me, dude."

Zac barely noticed his friend walk away, his attention focused on the gorgeous midwife with the warm green-gold eyes and even warmer heart. He'd agreed to help Carmen and he would. He'd go to her conference and play her besotted fiancé and keep his promise— because that was what he did. He wasn't his father. He was trustworthy, moral, strong. He'd play her perfect date, wine and dine her to within an inch of her life, fool her potential bosses, and help her get the job.

He'd keep his emotions and his past out of it.

And maybe, if he told himself that enough times, he'd start to believe it.

CHAPTER TWO

"UNITS RESPOND TO motor vehicle accident on Arctic Boulevard at West Fifty-Eighth Avenue. Thirty-seven-year-old female, eight months pregnant, complaining of chest pain. Over."

"Copy. FA14 responding," Zac said from behind the wheel. "Two minutes out."

He steered through the congested midday traffic toward the accident scene with lights blazing and sirens blaring, glad for something else to focus on besides Carmen. His weekend with her was only two days away now, and the closer the conference got the more worried he was that he'd made a horrible mistake.

What the hell had he been thinking, saying he'd pretend to be her fiancé in the last place in the world he ever wanted to set foot in again?

Besides the looming threat of being in his father's world again, there was also the fact that the connection between him and Carmen had never gone away after their one night together.

It wasn't even a conscious thing, really—more an underlying thread of awareness that pulled a bit tighter each time he was around her. In truth, it was why he hadn't dated anyone since they'd slept together. Much as he hated to admit it, since their fling he hadn't wanted anyone but her.

Which scared him more than just about anything else.

Because if he did get serious with her, what was to say it wouldn't end in betrayal, just like his father had betrayed his mother? Sure, his mother had found a way to forgive his father and work things out between them, but Zac couldn't expect the same from Carmen if he screwed up. Or *when* he screwed up, since the odds weren't in his favor given his genetics.

"What's got your drawers in a twist?" said Susan, his EMT partner, from the back of the rig as she readied their medical packs for the scene. "You've got that look again."

He glanced in the rearview mirror, scowling. "What look?"

"That brooding, pained one." Susan snorted. "Either that or you're constipated."

"Funny. *Not.*"

Zac sighed and shook his head, pulling in behind one of four squad cars at the accident scene and jamming the transmission into park. He was unbuckling his seat belt as he opened the door.

"I'm fine. Why are you so nosy?"

"Not any of my business," Susan said, climbing out at the back and handing him his pack. "Just figured you'd be a lot more cheerful since you have the whole upcoming weekend off. Lord knows I would be. I'd love to have three whole days to get away somewhere."

They weaved through the crowd of onlookers and cops to where three vehicles were crunched together and blocking two lanes—a flatbed truck in front, followed by a compact car, and finally a four-door sedan. Pretty clear from the damage and the placement that it had been a rear-end accident.

"Going anywhere special?" Susan asked him as they stopped near the middle car.

Yes.

"No." Zac dropped his pack on the ground near his feet and spoke to the cop in front of him. "EMT Zac Taylor. We got a call on a pregnant woman with chest pain?"

"Over here," the cop said, leading them around the vehicles to where two women stood near the curb, one perhaps around sixty, the other holding her very pregnant belly as she leaned against a lamppost. "That's her."

"I got it," Susan said, walking over to the pregnant woman.

Zac approached the older woman, who looked pale as death and was visibly shaking. "Were you involved in the accident, ma'am?"

She nodded. "Yes."

"This car?" He pointed to the middle car.

The woman raised a shaky hand toward the last vehicle. "That one."

"Are you hurt?"

"No…"

Her voice was barely more than a whisper and her trembling worsened as shock set in. She cradled her left hand and Zac noticed blood on one of her fingers, oozing from a fairly deep laceration.

The woman swayed slightly, and Zac grasped her arm to steady her. "Ma'am, how about I take you inside the ambulance and we see about getting your finger bandaged up? You can rest there a moment, okay?"

"She's pregnant…" the woman said, her voice dazed as he guided her toward the ambulance. "I want to make sure the baby's okay. I was driving behind her and she slammed on her brakes. I didn't realize I was so close and I went right into her."

Susan was already at the rig, getting the pregnant woman loaded onto a gurney. As he helped the older woman up the stairs into the back Zac caught snippets of what the woman was telling his partner.

"I was hit from behind and then pushed into the flatbed in front of me."

Given the damage to the vehicles, things could've been a lot worse for everyone, thought Zac.

He got the older woman situated on a bench in the rear of the rig, then climbed back out to help Susan load the gurney inside as well. Once both patients were secure, he tended to the older woman's lacerated finger while Susan checked the pregnant patient's vitals.

A bit of color had returned to the older woman's cheeks since she'd sat down and Zac handed her a cup of water. Her focus, though, remained fixated on the pregnant woman across from her, her expression anxious. "It all happened so fast. Then she got out and said the wheel had pushed into her stomach."

Zac glanced over to where Susan was hooking up a portable Doppler to the pregnant woman's stomach to monitor the fetal heart rate. A comforting *thump-thump* rhythm soon filled the interior of the ambulance. Susan looked up at him and hiked her chin to let him know everything sounded okay for now. They'd still transport the patient to the hospital, to make sure everything was fine, but it appeared she'd been lucky.

"Right," Zac said, finishing up with the bandage on the woman's finger. "This isn't as deep as I first thought, so you should be fine taking care of it at home, ma'am. Keep the wound clean and dry and change the dressing daily until it's healed. Any questions?"

The older woman shook her head.

"Okay, then." Zac stood. "You're done here. I believe the police officers outside might have a few questions for you."

"Blood pressure's one hundred and two over sixty-nine," Susan said, adjusting the cuff on the pregnant woman's arm.

"Is that good?" the other woman asked Zac.

"Fine. It's usually a bit low when you're pregnant." He helped the older woman stand, then led her toward the door. "Watch your step on the way down. I'll keep ahold of your arm until you're safely on the ground."

"Oh, wait," the woman said, stopping to turn back to the pregnant patient. "I'm so sorry about all this."

The pregnant woman nodded. "Thank you."

Once he'd gotten the older woman out of the

rig and over to the cops, Zac secured the rear doors on the ambulance, then climbed behind the wheel and radioed the ER to let them know they were coming.

"Anchorage Mercy, this is Frontier Ambulance Fourteen en route to your facility with a thirty-seven-year-old female who is thirty-eight weeks pregnant, involved in an MVA. Five minutes until arrival. Over."

"Copy. We'll have OB on standby," came the voice of a trauma nurse. "Any visible injuries?"

He glanced back at Susan in the rearview mirror.

"I have a midwife there," the pregnant woman said. "Carmen Sanchez. I want her present."

Zac nodded. Of course it would have to be Carmen.

He relayed the information, then signed off. "Be there soon. Over."

Thankfully, traffic was lighter now, and they pulled into the ambulance bay at the hospital in under six minutes. Zac and Susan unloaded their patient from the back, then wheeled the gurney through the automatic doors into the brightly lit ER.

As they headed down the hall toward one of the open trauma bays Zac gave the ER team a rundown from Susan's notes, doing his best to ignore the fact that Carmen was rushing along beside him, her arm brushing his and sending all sorts of inappropriate zings through his system.

"Patient states her abdomen struck the steering wheel hard during the accident. Fetal heart rate was normal during transport, no bleeding, spotting or cramping, though patient did complain of some chest pain post-accident. Patient has a history of three previous miscarriages and one stillbirth."

"Thank you. I'm familiar with her history," Carmen said, and she nudged him aside as they pushed the patient into an empty trauma bay where the OB on call, Dr. Tom Farber, raised a hand to Zac in greeting.

"We've got it from here."

The curtain abruptly swooshed closed in his face, and Zac stood there a moment, blinking at it, while Susan chuckled beside him.

"There's that look again, buddy." Susan clapped him on the back and chuckled. "Don't worry. Carmen's too good for you anyway. I'm going back out to the rig to clean up."

Zac moved over to the nurses' station to get out of the way. He didn't usually hang around after they'd dropped off patients, but things had been slow all day and his shift was almost over.

Besides, he wanted to make sure things were all right with the baby.

That was the excuse he was going with anyway.

"You're still here?" Carmen said when she emerged from behind the curtain twenty minutes later.

The words had emerged snarkier than she'd intended—but *darn it*. Bad enough that she hadn't been able to sleep well since their conversation in the cafeteria, her mind whirling with thoughts of him. Now he was distracting her at work too. The only way her plan was going to work was if she kept her wits about her and her feelings out of it. In fact, most things in life worked better that way, in her experience. Caring too much only meant trouble.

She stepped around Zac, who stood far too close for her comfort. The weekend conference was approaching fast. And, as if that weren't stressful enough, she'd just worked three twelve-hour shifts in a row and now, with this new patient's arrival, her already long night was about to become even longer.

"Figured you'd have a hot date or something."

"No dates for me. I'm off the market now, remember?"

She gave him a pointed glance. If Zac had

taken offense at her snapping at him, he didn't show it. He just stood there, grinning and looking smug.

"Just getting into practice for my role this weekend. Besides, my shift's almost done. And since when do you care so much about my schedule?"

"I don't care," Carmen lied. "I just don't want any rumors starting around here about us. You know how people gossip."

Zac snorted. "You don't think they're going to hear about it from Priya and Lance anyway? The guy's my good friend, but I don't tell him anything I don't want the rest of the hospital to know. He's worse than social media when it comes to privacy."

He laughed, but she gave him a dark look. "Don't remind me."

"Hey, this was *your* idea, remember?" he said, leaning closer.

Close enough that his warm breath ghosted the shell of her ear and made her shiver.

"Speaking of remembering—I've been thinking about that night we spent together. I remember those soft little sounds you made when I held you close. The way you gasped and sighed when I kissed that sensitive spot on your neck… the one near your collarbone where…"

The sound of a clearing throat had her jerking away from Zac. Good thing too, since her pulse was throbbing in her ears and her skin felt too tight for her body. As if the memories she had of that night weren't naughty enough, now she had to think about Zac reliving them too. Lord, help her. When had it got so hot in here?

Carmen swallowed hard and looked over her shoulder to see Tom standing outside the trauma bay as she tugged at her collar.

"Sorry," Tom said, glancing between her and Zac. "Didn't mean to interrupt."

"You weren't," Carmen answered, too fast. After smoothing her hand down the front of her pink scrubs, she raised her chin. "What's your assessment, Doctor?"

"I think she's good to go. No signs of fetal distress. Baby's heart rate is normal and strong. Mother's blood pressure is fine too." He walked over to the counter. "No spotting or cervical effacement on exam. I'd say she's fine to discharge—unless you disagree."

"Agreed. Excellent."

Carmen was doing her best to portray her usual efficient self, even though her insides were still fluttering from Zac's heated flirtation. Lord help her… If one brief encounter with him had her this riled up, she was in big trouble for the weekend ahead.

"I'll go in and talk to her for a bit…answer

any questions she might have…then send her on her way. Thank you, Dr. Farber."

"My pleasure." Tom gave her and Zac one more assessing look before backing away toward the elevators. "You kids have fun."

"We will, thanks," Zac said, raising his hand.

"No, we won't." Carmen gave him a narrowed stare. "Fun is the last thing we'll be having this weekend."

"Remind me again why I'm going, then?" He raised a brow at her, then sighed. "I know… To help out a friend. Got it. Trust me. This won't be a party for me either."

It was her turn to snort now. "Really? Why not? Free stay at a luxury resort, all expenses paid? Sounds like a great time to me."

When he didn't answer right away she looked up from the paperwork she was filling out and noticed his playful expression had turned serious.

"What?"

"Nothing. It's not important."

He looked away and she saw the shadow of something cross his handsome face. Before she could ask about it though, one of the nurses came up to the desk and started talking to him.

Carmen felt a quick pinch of unaccountable jealousy before she pushed it aside. She had no claim on Zac Taylor. He was helping her out this weekend. That was all.

She sighed and returned to her documentation, doing her best to ignore Zac and failing miserably. Seeing Tom and Wendy so happy together with their new baby, plus Tom's daughter Sam from his previous marriage, had given Carmen hope that she'd find the same for herself someday—if she ever found the time to date again in her busy schedule.

Until then she was stuck with fake fiancés and imaginary lovers.

Exhaling slowly, Carmen signed off on the patient's discharge papers and handed them to the nurse, telling her to let the patient know she'd be in momentarily to answer her questions, then continued scribbling on the patient's chart.

Zac remained steadfastly beside her, and she gave him a side glance and rubbed her stiff neck. "Don't you have another EMS run to go on, or something?"

"It's Tuesday. Things are slow. Susan and I are just hanging out until the clock runs down or another call comes in."

Her stupid neck cramped again and she winced, cursing softly.

"Here." He brushed her hand aside, massaging the knots in her neck and upper shoulders with those long, strong fingers of his. Between the heat of his body behind her, penetrating her scrubs, and the heavenly feel of his talented digits easing away her tension, Carmen nearly melted into a puddle of goo at the man's feet. Good thing she had the desk there to hold her up.

"You shouldn't push yourself so hard."

She scoffed. "I push myself because that's what it takes to survive."

"Last time I checked this was Alaska, not the apocalypse."

"You never know when things could fall apart. Slack off and you could lose everything."

She closed her eyes as he worked on a particularly sore spot between her shoulder blades with his thumbs, leaving her feeling far too relaxed and vulnerable.

Reluctantly, Carmen forced herself to step away from him. "Besides, I've got more than myself to provide for."

"Hmm? Tell me more about that," Zac said, leaning against the counter once more. "I know we're exchanging fact sheets, but if we're going to pretend to be in love I'd like to hear about your family and your responsibilities from you. What's important to you should seem important to me if we want this to be believable."

The reminder of the upcoming weekend was

like a glass of icy water to her face. Carmen straightened and moved out from under his touch. She had to keep her head and be cool, calm, and rational about this if she wanted to succeed.

"My mother and my sister live with me. My mother is ill and requires round-the-clock care. My sister is trying to get into the nursing program at the University of Alaska after she graduates from high school in May. Both things are expensive. This new job in California pays more money and has more responsibility. That's all you need to know for now. If you'll excuse me? I need to go back in with my patient. Unlike you, I still have several hours left on my shift."

She started to walk away, only to have him tag along next to her.

Damn. Hopefully he'd drop the subject of her private life. She didn't like talking about herself. She especially didn't like feeling such a strong attraction to a man who made her want to open up to him, made her want to confide in him and lean on him. All of that was completely unacceptable.

Men were unreliable. Her father had taught her that lesson the day he'd walked out on them, leaving her poor mother to work three jobs just to keep a roof over their heads. Because of that, Carmen had virtually raised her little sister Clara.

Forget childhood. She'd had to grow up quickly. The more self-reliant she was, the better.

Perhaps her upbringing was the reason midwifery suited her so well. Well, that and the fact that her patients needed her. Carmen liked to be needed. She was used to being needed, no matter the time involved or the personal cost. When a call for help came in she shut off her feelings and got the job done.

Which was just as well because messy emotions only got in the way.

Instead of heading back into the trauma bay she continued on around the corner, deciding to burn off a little energy before speaking with her patient again. The nurse would be busy going over the discharge papers anyway.

They reached the stairwell and Carmen stopped, pushing open the door.

"I thought you were going to see your patient?" Zac said.

"I am—in a minute." Carmen's phone buzzed in her pocket and she pulled it out. "Need to take this phone call first."

Not exactly true. But if she didn't get away from Zac soon she was liable to do something stupid—like push him up against the wall and have her wicked way with him.

He continued to stand there, staring at her, looking far too gorgeous for his own good, which annoyed her to no end. "Anything else I can do for you?"

Zac opened his mouth and then closed it, as if reconsidering his words. He backed away slightly. "It's okay to let people in sometimes."

"Seriously?" She laughed and shook her head, doing her best to sound flippant. "Maybe you should take your own advice, then, mister, instead of shutting me down each time I ask a personal question about *you*. See you later, Zac."

"Is that a challenge?" he called from behind her. "I love a challenge."

Carmen chuckled as the door closed behind her, leaving her alone in the stairwell. She leaned back against the wall, her heart still pounding and her mind still racing.

Silly. So silly. Just infatuation. That was all her reaction was.

She closed her eyes and took a deep breath to calm herself—only to have more images of their one night together flash through her head. The two of them entwined in her sheets…him bringing her to release again and again as she cried out his name in ecstasy.

No matter how drunk she'd been that night, a girl didn't forget something that good.

Weys, dat boy rel bess...

The Trinidadian slang echoed in Carmen's head. And it wasn't wrong.

Zac was really sexy. Sexy times a thousand. Sexy times infinity and beyond.

She was in trouble and the conference hadn't even started yet.

Hands shaking, Carmen pulled out her cell phone and called her sister back as she climbed the stairs to the third floor.

Clara picked up on the second ring. *"Ey, wam?"*

"I might have done something incredibly stupid. That's what's up."

Before she could stop the words, an explanation of her fake engagement and the upcoming weekend with Zac tumbled out of her. She felt like she had to tell someone or else she'd burst.

"Wait—wait!" Clara said, as the sound of their mother's favorite soap opera droned on in the background. "You did *what*?"

"I lied to my potential new employer in California. They're very pro-family, and they were so impressed with Priya and her engagement to Lance I felt like I had to make something up in order to still have a shot at the job. I *need* this promotion, sis. *We* need this promotion. The extra money would pay for Mama's care and help put you through university."

Carmen stopped on the landing between the second and third floors, trying to convince herself as much as her sister that she'd done the right thing.

"Look, it's no big deal, right? Three days of pretending and then it's over and hopefully I get the job. Easy."

"What about leaving Alaska? I thought you liked it here. *I* like it here," Clara said.

"I do like Anchorage," said Carmen.

She loved Anchorage the same as Mama and her sister did. She'd hate to leave. But that was beside the point. You did what you needed to do.

"California is pretty too, though. If I get the job it will be like we're living on the island again. Beaches and sunshine and the ocean. They have good nursing programs at their colleges too."

"Hmm…" Clara didn't sound convinced, but it was too late to back out now. "And you think taking this man you had a fling with and having him pretend to be your fiancé will get you this new job? After you two…you know…?"

Yeah, she'd told her sister about the one-night stand. Hard to hide a man staying over in your bed when you shared the same living space. *Ugh.* Clara was right. Whatever had made her think inviting Zac to be her fake fiancé was the most brilliant decision ever?

In the end, though, what choice had she had? With Priya's stellar background and experience, Carmen needed to produce someone who could seriously schmooze. Priya's family was rich, and she'd had the best education and training money could buy. Carmen had worked nights and weekends to pay for her RN degree at the University of the Southern Caribbean.

After that she'd scraped together enough money from tips at the bar and working third shift at a twenty-four-hour convenience clinic to move her family from Trinidad to Anchorage, where she'd interned at Anchorage Mercy and completed her graduate degree.

Then she'd sat for the national certification exam and applied for her Advanced Nurse Practitioner license. The whole process had taken a decade, but it had meant a more secure future for the ones she loved and she'd do it all again, if asked.

Carmen said at last, "Zac knows the score."

"Does he?" Clara said, her tone skeptical. "I don't want you to get your heart broken."

Carmen didn't want that either. Problem was, she'd never really had a Plan B when it came to this weekend. And, honestly, their mutual attraction might be a *good* thing if they could keep to the script and use it to their advantage, making their ruse more believable. Lord knew their chemistry was still sizzling hot, despite the fact months had passed since they'd done the deed.

"I'll be fine—promise," she said, to convince herself as much as Clara.

She pushed away from the wall and squared her shoulders before walking out of the stairwell again. The hallway was delightfully empty, thank goodness.

"You're all set to take care of Mama this weekend?"

Clara sighed. "Yep."

Regret pinched Carmen's chest. She hated to ask her little sister to care for their mother, but it couldn't be helped in this situation. She wanted Clara to experience all the things she'd never had at her age—parties and fun and boyfriends and dating and all of life's good things.

"What time's your flight?" Clara asked.

"We fly out Thursday morning. Zac's meeting me at the airport." Carmen picked at her nails—a bad habit that tended to recur when she was stressed. "On a private jet."

"*Weys!* Well, try to have a good time this weekend. You deserve to let loose. Just not too much, eh?"

"Don't worry. It's still a working midwifery

conference." Carmen laughed. "Mama doing all right?"

"She's fine. Watching her *telenovela*."

"Good. Okay. I need to go. Tell her I love her and I'll see her later tonight."

Carmen ended the call and headed back into the busy ER. She'd hoped her little walk would help clear her mind and sort out her thoughts. Instead, it had only brought more concerns to the surface.

If she was honest, her sister had touched on something she feared herself. Not that she and Zac wouldn't be able to fool people into thinking they were a couple, but that Carmen wouldn't be able to stop fooling herself into believing they were…

CHAPTER THREE

LATE THURSDAY MORNING, Zac took a moment to collect himself as he stepped into the ticketing area of Ted Stevens Anchorage International Airport. There were, of course, dozens of people milling about, but his eyes went immediately to a petite beauty with glowing mocha skin and copper-streaked curls, standing on the other side of the security gate, checking her watch.

Dressed in jeans, an emerald-green turtleneck, a black parka and black suede boots, Carmen looked a far cry from the way she looked dressed in her usual scrubs at the hospital. Younger and way sexier, if that were possible.

Whoa, cowboy.

He took a deep breath and reminded himself why he was here. This wasn't a vacation. This wasn't about sex. This was *work*.

After going through the security checkpoint, he strode toward her, coming up on the side opposite to where she was looking.

"Sorry I'm late," he said, setting his leather carry-on bag on the floor near his feet.

She turned and looked him up and down, checked her watch again, then took off for the nearby escalators, calling to him over her shoulder as she went. "You *are* late. I hope this isn't a sign of how the rest of the weekend will go. And you're also overdressed."

"I wasn't sure what to wear. We didn't discuss that," he muttered, racing after her and catching her up near the end of the concourse, feeling uncomfortable now in his dark jeans and tweed blazer, with the open collar of his white dress shirt suddenly too confining for comfort. "You already have the gate number?"

"Don't need one," she said to him over her shoulder. "Private jet, remember?"

"Right." Zac nodded, feeling even more like an idiot. He knew that. Should've remembered from the days traveling with his father.

He forced his attention away from the seductive sway of Carmen's hips as she walked slightly in front of him and focused straight ahead instead.

Mind on the game, buddy.

A flight attendant waited for them near a side door and escorted them out onto the chilly tarmac, where Zac got his first view of the plane, which was similar to the one his father had owned when Zac was growing up. The knots in his gut tightened.

They approached the small, sleek white aircraft with the fancy logo of the California clinic painted on its tail. Whoever owned that clinic certainly had cash in the bank. These things carried a sixty-five to seventy-million-dollar price tag. Flew like a dream too.

Back in the day, before his father's betrayal had caused the world Zac knew to crash down around him, he'd logged enough flight hours to become a pilot himself. But that had been another life—a different Zac.

"Here we are," the flight attendant said, stopping at the bottom of a set of steps. "Enjoy your flight."

"Thank you."

Carmen climbed the steps in front of him and Zac did his best not to notice how her jeans cupped her cute butt perfectly. She stopped just before the top and turned to face him. Distracted, he nearly collided right into her. Good thing he had a firm grip on the railing, otherwise he might have had to grab her to keep his balance. And touching her at this point, even for safety reasons, would be a big mistake.

"Ready for this?" she asked. "Did you bring your dossier?"

He squinted up at her in the sunshine and

avoided staring at the gold cross necklace nestled atop her bosom. "I am. I did. Did you?"

She inhaled deep, then nodded. "Yes. We can go over them during the flight. I was hoping you'd be on time so we could do it beforehand. I think Priya and Lance have already boarded."

Damn. He'd wanted to get here sooner too, but Susan had called him with some questions about the inventory, and then he'd gotten wrapped up in packing, and there'd been road construction, and now it seemed like everything was conspiring against him today.

If he didn't know better, he'd take it as a sign that he shouldn't be here at all. Too late now, though.

"We'll just have to bluff our way through," she said.

Bluffing he could do. He might not have a good poker face, but he could BS with the best of them. Another dubious skill he'd picked up from his father.

Zac stepped up on the next stair, putting him and Carmen level. This close, he caught a hint of her jasmine perfume and her heat penetrated his cotton shirt, making his fingertips itch to pull her closer.

To keep himself from reaching for her, he jammed his hand into his jacket pocket instead and pulled out the ring he'd purchased and stashed there earlier.

Zac held Carmen's gaze as he took her left hand and slid it on her finger. "Need this if we're going to make it believable, eh?"

When she didn't respond, he glanced up to find her staring down at the single solitaire round-cut diamond set in platinum. He'd gone for the real thing, thinking it would fool even the most persistent of doubters at the resort. He'd return it once they got back. No big deal.

"Let's do this."

Carmen bit her bottom lip. "It's beautiful…"

"Beautiful ring for a beautiful woman."

He winked, then waited until she'd turned around again before nudging her toward the door of the plane. If they didn't get off these steps soon he'd be running the risk of sweeping her into his arms and kissing her right there. Which was bad. So, *so* bad. They hadn't even left Anchorage yet and he was already having a hard time not imagining all the naughty things he wanted to do to her…with her. Same as he'd done that long-ago night…

Damn.

The good news came as soon as they boarded the aircraft. Lance and Priya gaped at their arrival, stunned and speechless. The bad news was that their silence didn't last.

"Dude!" Lance looked at the sparkling ring on Carmen's finger, then up at Zac. "I was right! No wonder you didn't tell me what you were doing this weekend. Sly dog!"

"I wasn't sure until the last minute that I could make it. And, yes, Carmen and I are together. You were right. Congrats," Zac said, tucking his leather bag in an overhead bin, then taking a seat beside Carmen in a cushy leather chair and buckling his seat belt. "I had to do some schedule-wrangling at work, but anything to spend more time with my snuggle-bug, here. Isn't that right, sweetheart?"

At his use of the endearment a small muscle near the corner of Carmen's eye began to twitch. He reached over and clasped her icy hand in his. She covered it quickly and forced a tight smile.

"Yes, that's right, *doux-doux*."

At his raised brow, she squeezed his hand.

"Zac and I have been searching for ways to spend more time together outside of work and I thought this weekend was a perfect opportunity. What with all the stress of planning a wedding and all."

"Okay. Wait a minute. You're telling me that you two have not only been dating but that you're *engaged*? How the hell did you keep this secret from everyone?" Priya asked, her expression skeptical. "We work together. I see you more than your own family does. And I didn't have a clue. I didn't even know you were dating anyone since Jeff, let alone Zac."

Zac was pretty sure he'd lost all circulation in his fingers. Carmen was holding his hand so tight, and the stupid diamond was cutting into his skin, but he'd signed on for this and he intended to make sure the weekend was a success.

He kissed Carmen's cold hand and tucked it near his heart, milking the moment for all it was worth. "We purposely kept it under wraps. You know how brutal the rumor mill at the hospital is, and my Carmen loves her privacy. Plus, we wanted to make sure things were solid between us before announcing it to the world."

Lance watched him closely, gaze narrowed. "But you never once mentioned it to me either, and I'm your best friend. In fact, I've never even *seen* you two together, except for that crazy holiday party. Wait! Did you two hook up that night? You did, didn't you?" Lance leaned forward, his gaze darting between Zac and Carmen. "Well, I'll be damned. And you're okay with moving to California if she gets this job, huh? Never thought I'd see the day you'd leave your beloved Alaska."

Uncomfortable heat rose beneath the collar of Zac's shirt, but he resisted the urge to fidget. Lance was right—both about him and Carmen hooking up and about Zac leaving Anchorage. The thought of moving away from his beautiful home state felt like a punch in the gut. Still, he needed to play along, because that was what he'd agreed when he'd signed on for Carmen's weekend of deception.

Besides, having a grain of truth mixed in with the lies should make them more believable. And the fact that he knew *that*—again courtesy of his father—made him even more queasy. His gut cramped and disgust flooded his bloodstream.

This is not the same. I'm not like him. Not at all.

He was only pretending in order to help out a friend, to help someone he cared for.

Never mind that his father had claimed the same reasons—said he'd lied to protect Zac and his mother, said it had only happened one time.

Old memories and pain rose, threatening to overtake him if he didn't get up, get off this plane, get back home where he'd be safe.

Thankfully a flight attendant came to make sure they were prepared for takeoff and to get their drink orders. The captain announced on the PA that they were completing their preflight checks and that once they received clearance from the tower they should be airborne.

Zac took a few much-needed deep breaths

and concentrated on the in-flight safety checklist a second attendant was going over with
them.

By the time the first flight attendant returned
with their beverages he was back to normal
again. Or about as close as he was going to get
on this trip. It helped that Lance and Priya had
been directed to swivel their chairs forward during takeoff, giving him and Carmen a reprieve
from their inquisition—at least for now.

Zac exhaled, glad the spotlight was off him
for the moment. They taxied down the runway,
Carmen still hanging on to his hand for dear
life.

He wondered if she was a nervous traveler.
They'd never really discussed it. They'd never
really discussed a lot of things.

Zac turned slightly to glance her way and
lowered his voice. "That seemed to go about as
well as could be expected."

She released his hand at last and took a long
drink of her wine. "Yeah? You looked like you
were going to throw up there for a minute when
Lance was grilling you."

"I'm fine. Considering we didn't prep what
we were going to say ahead of time, it just threw
me a bit off-kilter, that's all."

Liar.

He looked over to where Lance and Priya

faced away from them, their heads together, most likely discussing their impromptu engagement.

The fact was, the prospect of heading straight back into the lion's den was shaking him more than he cared to admit. His mother might have been the bigger person and forgiven his father, but Zac hadn't been able to do the same. It had broken her heart, but he'd left out of respect for her. He loved his mother more than anything, and he hadn't wanted to disrupt her life further by constantly arguing and fighting with his father, so he'd gone.

He missed her every day, though—and, much as he liked to think he'd gotten over the hurt a long time ago, perhaps it wasn't as far behind him as he pretended.

As soon as the seat belt light went off he unbuckled and shifted in his seat. "Where's your dossier? I want to be prepared the next time those two come at us."

He stood and pulled his own dossier out of his bag in the overhead bin and handed it to her. It had seemed stupid to put his paltry list of ten things in a binder, but he didn't want Lance and Priya to see it accidentally.

"It's not much, but it's all I can share with you."

"*All* you can share?" She opened the binder

and looked at the paper inside, then back at him. "Are you working for the CIA?"

"No. There are just things about me that I don't tell people."

"I'm not *people*," she whispered. "I'm supposed to be your fiancée."

"Fake fiancée," he corrected. "Look, this flight's only an hour. Maybe now would be a good time for you to fill me in on your list and anything else you think I should know."

She finished off her wine, then reached into the tote near her feet and pulled out her own folder, which she handed to him. "Unlike you, I have no secrets. Everything about me is on there."

He read her papers, then raised a brow. "You even wrote a meet-cute for us? I'd been chasing after you for years and you finally took pity on me?"

"It's better than the truth, yeah? Which Lance has already guessed, darn him." She reached into her bag again and pulled out a pair of reading glasses. He raised an eyebrow "What? Working on all those charts makes my eyes tired."

He snorted. "Sure. I like them. Makes you look like a sexy librarian."

"Don't get any ideas, mister."

"Can't help it when I'm around you."

Carmen gave an aggrieved sigh. "Save the flirting for when it counts, okay? It's wasted on me now."

"But it wasn't back then, was it?" He laughed, resting his head back against the seat. "Do you remember that night? I do. That little red dress you wore...with the neckline down to there and the split up to—"

"Stop it." She smacked his arm. "It wasn't that bad. Besides, you weren't much better, Mr. Tight-Jeans-and-T-shirt. Looking all sexy on the dance floor."

"You thought I was sexy, huh?" He waggled his brows. "You were the sexy one. Shaking your booty. And, man, when we slow-danced." He sighed and closed his eyes. "I can't hear that song now without thinking of you."

She chuckled. "What was it again? Oh, right. 'Havana' by Camila Cabello."

He shifted slightly, knowing he was treading on dangerous ground by flirting with her, but unable to stop himself. A night didn't go by when he didn't remember her at that party, looking like heaven on earth in that dress, holding her, kissing her, making love to her all night long.

"You were scorching hot, lady."

"You weren't so bad yourself, mister."

She turned her head to look at him, her full

lips parted and her eyes sparkling with heat. Then the attendant stopped by to refill their drinks and the spell was broken.

Carmen faced forward and frowned down at his dossier. "Best concentrate on this right now. Like you said, the flight's only an hour."

Right.

Zac straightened and went back to memorizing the stuff on her papers. Father deserted the family when Carmen was just a kid...raised by a single mother...caregiver for her younger sister...worked her way through nursing school. No wonder they got along so well. They were very much alike. Well, except for the father leaving part. Unfortunately, his father was still right where he'd started.

Zac had been the one to do the leaving.

"So, tell me what's not on here."

She gave him a side-glance and a frown. "I told you—it's all on there."

"One thing isn't."

"What's that?"

She crossed her arms, drawing his attention to her breasts before he looked away fast. Apparently not fast enough, though, if her perturbed look was any indication.

"Why did you choose *me* to bring this weekend?" he asked around the sudden constriction in his throat.

Because *darn* if more memories of that night after the holiday party weren't shoving their way into his brain. How her soft curves had felt in his palms, the way she'd sighed and held him closer, how he'd taken her taut nipple into his mouth and licked and sucked gently…

Nope. Nope, nope, nope.

Not going there. Not now and definitely not later.

Keep it together.

Carmen was the opposite of the kind of woman he normally slept with. Usually he went for girls who liked to party. Women who weren't looking for more than a night or two and then left with a fond farewell. Carmen had *forever* written all over her, even if she denied it.

Knowing she wasn't his type should be making keeping his distance this weekend easier. Except it wasn't.

"I told you that day in the cafeteria. You're a friend. I trust you. We have chemistry, and I thought that would make this whole charade easier. Don't read more into it than is actually there." She scanned his list again. "You're a Capricorn? I would've guessed Leo, or maybe Scorpio."

"Scorpio, huh?" he said, going along with her explanation for now, even though his gut told him there was more to her reason for asking him than she was letting on. "How's that?"

"Because you obviously like your secrets."

"I don't like secrets. What I like is privacy. I've seen from experience how rash decisions can hurt people and I—"

"Aw...trouble in paradise already?" a female voice interrupted.

Zac looked over to find Priya and Lance had turned toward them again, clearly ready for a new round of questions.

Yeah. It was going to be a very long weekend.

"So, spill the beans," Lance said, focusing his laser-like attention on Carmen. "How did you two get together? How long has it been going on? Mostly, how in the hell did you manage to keep it a secret so long?"

"Oh, well—" Zac started.

But Carmen held up a hand to stop him.

"We hooked up at the hospital holiday party and we saw each other off and on after that. Things got more serious recently and we got engaged."

"Really?" Priya narrowed her gaze and crossed her arms. "That quick?"

"When the love bug bites..." Carmen said, stiffening slightly beside him.

"That's odd...because just last month you told me you had no intention of getting involved with anyone. You said your career and your family were too important to you and took up too much of your time. Did that change?"

"No." Carmen frowned down at her hands in her lap and fiddled with the zip on her down vest. "I mean, yes. I mean, perhaps I just had a change of perspective. Meeting the right person can do that to you."

"Hmm…" Priya looked completely unconvinced. "Is this about the job? Are you faking this to try and get the job at the California clinic?"

Zac coughed to cover his surprised laugh. Nothing like having your ruse ruined before it had even started. "No. Of course not."

"Don't be ridiculous. My qualifications speak for themselves—as do yours. I don't need a man to win a job." Carmen lifted her chin defiantly. "Zac is here because we're in love and because this weekend is a chance for us to spend some quality time together away from the hospital. That's it. Right, *doux-doux*? 'Every bread have a cheese,' as my mama says."

"What?" Zac scrunched his nose.

"'Every bread have a cheese'," Carmen said. "It's an old Trinidadian saying. Every person is bound to find a soul mate. And Zac is mine."

He barely had time to nod before she kissed him soundly.

Her lips were just as sweet and soft against his as he remembered. Dangerous, that, since talk of soul mates wasn't in his vocabulary anymore. Still, he'd just begun to lose himself in the moment, cupping her cheeks to keep her close, when Lance cleared his throat.

"Dude, get a room," his buddy said, breaking them apart.

"Dude, we are," Zac countered, sitting back, but keeping hold of Carmen's hand, lacing his fingers through her chilled ones, hoping to convey some strength and solidarity through the gesture.

A beep sounded through the cabin and he glanced up.

"The seat belt signs are lit up again. You two better turn around and buckle up. It could get bumpy."

Priya gave them both another pointed stare before slowly turning her chair around to face forward. Lance followed suit, giving Zac and Carmen a small modicum of privacy again.

"Okay?" he whispered, turning his head to look at her.

Her full lips were compressed into a thin line and he had the urge to kiss her again, just to get her to relax. But he thought better of it. Talking seemed like a safer option at this point, given the way his blood pounded and his heart still slammed against his chest.

"Hey, don't worry about them. We can avoid them once we get to the resort. We got this."

She didn't look convinced at all.

"Tell me some more about this job. Why now?"

She gave a small shrug, staring out the window beside her. "I've been at Anchorage Mercy for nearly a decade now. I have a chance for something bigger and I'm taking it."

"Because of the money?"

Ambition and money, he understood. He'd grown up around enough of it. Another reason his life in Anchorage suited him. Laid-back, straightforward. No fuss, no muss. No lies and betrayal. Well, present situation excluded.

He sipped his ale straight from the bottle and watched her over the rim. "You'd be a manager at this new clinic in Big Sur?"

"Yes—if I get the job. I've worked hard my entire life and I don't want to risk losing what I've gained. That's why it's important we avoid any...complications."

"Complications?" Zac blinked, considering that a second.

He assumed she meant sex. But in his mind sex wasn't complicated. Commitment was the real complication.

Commitment couldn't be trusted. Commitment was made to be broken.

He'd learned that lesson the hard way, thanks to his father.

They sat in silence for a while, Carmen flipping through a magazine while Zac napped. Finally Carmen nudged him with her elbow and he straightened, scrubbing a hand over his face to clear his fuzzy head.

"What? Did I miss something?"

"No." She chuckled, and the sound seemed to brighten the interior of the cabin. "You were snoring."

"Was not." He frowned. "You're just saying that because it was on my sheet."

"One of the very few things on there." She set her magazine aside and turned her attention to him again. "There's nothing on there about your family or your past."

"It's not important."

"I disagree." Carmen shifted slightly, settling back into the corner of her seat to face him. "Family is everything. It shapes us, defines us—it's our beginning and our end."

"Very poetic."

Her foot bumped his and a fresh zing of awareness zipped through his system. He looked away and took a large swig of ale to get his damn fool head back on straight.

"My dad's a businessman and my mom stays home. My father runs his own company. We had a falling out. I haven't spoken to either of them in years. My family is the last thing I want defining me. I'm my own man."

"Whatever you say. But the fact you cut them out of your life and won't speak about them is telling me a lot about you right there." Her gaze met his and held.

Zac coughed and straightened in his seat. "Drop it."

"Fine. For now." She lowered her voice. "But eventually you're going to have to tell me more, in case it comes up at the reception tonight. My potential new bosses will be there. Besides, I've laid myself bare for you."

"Bare?"

The images that word conjured were triple X. She'd leaned in, close enough for her warm breath to fan his face, and the sweet scent of her perfume surrounded him. A few millimeters more and he could kiss her again, taste her, see if she was as delicious the second time around…

The plane hit a pocket of turbulence, jarring them hard.

"Please be sure your seat belts are fastened," the flight attendant said, passing by.

Carmen sat back, pushing the curls away from her flushed face. "Dammit."

"What's wrong?"

She shook her head and gave a rueful smile, staring out the window, away from him. *"Yuh cyah play mas if yuh fraid powder."*

"Sorry?" Zac frowned as he fastened his seat belt. "Is that more Trinidadian?"

"Yes. It means don't get involved in something if you can't handle the danger."

Touché.

"Dangerous" seemed the correct word for the heat shimmering between them. Their chemistry had always been hot and volatile, ready to boil over at any second. Which had been fine back in Anchorage, because they'd both been able to escape easily. Now, though, they were stuck on a plane, somewhere over the frozen Yukon, with no way out but through even if their choice to fake an engagement this weekend had been a bad one.

Frustrated in more ways than one, Carmen sat facing away from Zac for as long as she could—until she got a crick in her neck and her butt was numb from staying in the same spot so long.

This weekend clearly wasn't going to be as cut-and-dried as she'd planned, especially as her whole body tingled and her breath caught each time she locked eyes with the man. Yes, they were supposed to act like a couple for the next three days, but it was supposed to be *pretend*.

This connection between them felt all too real.

If the plane hadn't bumped them around earlier she would've kissed him again. Would've done a lot more too, if they'd been alone. She wanted him. Intensely. Like she'd never wanted anything *ever*.

Which made no sense. Carmen was a sensible person. She didn't go around acting on her impulses, didn't throw caution to the wind. She was the stable one, the caregiver, the person other people depended on. No matter how gorgeous Zac was, or how he made want throb through her like molten lava, she could not let him overwhelm her good sense.

She'd lived her whole life putting others before herself, always biding her time. But she wasn't a hermit. She dated. She went out with people. She socialized. But she never let things get too deep. Because all men left in the end.

Her last long-term relationship before loser Jeff had lasted two years. Until Steve had moved on to greener and less complicated pastures. He'd told her they just didn't want the same things, but deep down inside Carmen feared she knew the truth. She didn't deserve love. After all, maybe if she'd been better, smarter, more amenable and less driven, Steve would have stayed. Her father too.

She sighed and gazed out at the fluffy clouds below them. Now that the time had arrived to go after this clinic job she felt torn. Part of her didn't want to miss her shot—the ambitious part of her that always made her feel like she had to prove her worth through her accomplishments. But another part of her felt scared and sad that she was willing to lie in order to get the position.

Not that there was much she could do about it now, at thirty-thousand feet, with Zac in the seat next to her.

There was nothing to do now but make the best of it.

Never mind that he kissed like the devil and tasted like sinful desire…

"This is just pretend," she whispered aloud. "We're friends. We don't want to risk that."

"Agreed," Zac said, not looking at her.

"We have to work together at the hospital. No sense making things awkward."

"Nope."

"Okay. So…" She exhaled slowly and stared up at the cabin ceiling. "Just pretend."

He closed her folder and turned to her once more. "I'll ask again. Tell me about this job."

She looked at him, surprised. "You want to hear about the position in California? Now?"

"No." Zac gave her a flat stare. "What I actually want is to finish that kiss we started a few minutes ago. But since I can't…"

She sucked in a quick breath and forced herself to concentrate on the details of the new managerial position up for grabs at the California clinic, hoping the business talk would chill her ardor.

"The person they hire will oversee a staff of four midwives, with the possible addition of more as the practice grows. And they'll be in charge of training too."

Zac's tense shoulders relaxed a bit. "Sounds right up your alley."

"Yes. I plan to present a framework to assist midwives in developing a consistent approach to screening for perinatal mood and anxiety disorders to the owners while at the conference."

She hadn't spoken to anyone but her sister about her plan, but it might be good to practice her spiel on him before her presentation to her potential new bosses at the conference.

"I'd also like to develop interventions and strategies for referral, response to emergent situations, and following up to ensure continuity of care."

"Wow," he said, his tone impressed. "That's great."

"Thanks. Let's hope the owners think so too."

Carmen checked her watch. Less than half an hour until landing. Nervousness buzzed through her system like a swarm of restless bees.

She stared at her hands in her lap. "Listen, all reminiscing aside, I don't normally have one-night stands like we did after that party."

"I know." Zac glanced over at her.

"You do?"

He sighed. "You didn't have the confidence of a serial bed-hopper."

"Oh."

Zac handed his empty beer bottle to a passing attendant, then faced her. "It's not a bad thing."

"Right…" Heat prickled her cheeks and she quickly changed the subject. "Want to look at my magazine?"

"Sure." He laughed, staring down at the cover. "'How to pick the best lipstick based on your astrological sign'?"

"What?" She shrugged. "I didn't want anything too heavy."

"Well, you got that, then." He made a face as he flipped through the pages. "Seriously?"

She glanced at the overhead bin above their head, thinking of his lone bag. "Um… Zac?"

"Yeah?"

"Is that bag the only luggage you brought?"

"Yeah." He flipped a page. "Why?"

"Did you remember to bring a tux for the evening parties?"

Not that she didn't appreciate his current ensemble, which clung to every muscle and sinew of his chiseled torso.

"Oh, yeah. I had the rest of my stuff sent on ahead to the resort." He flipped another page. "Figured it would be easier that way."

"Huh…" She hadn't even considered doing that, and the fact *he* had gave her pause. "I didn't know that was a thing."

"People do it all the time. Business travelers, mainly, though sometimes other people too. Resorts usually have staff who will make sure the luggage gets to the right room after the guests check in."

He glanced up at her then, as if realizing he'd said too much, then looked away again fast.

"At least that's what I've heard."

"Interesting…" She watched him more closely. "What business did you say your father was in?"

"I didn't." He handed her back the magazine. "Nice try, though."

"C'mon. You'll have to trust me eventually."

"No, I won't. This is just a weekend, remember? Besides, I'm Julia Roberts here."

"I'm sorry?" She gave him a confused look.

"Julia Roberts? In *Pretty Woman*?" He grinned. "I'm your fake date. Your beck-and-call girl. Or guy, in this case. Now, give me your credit card so I can go on the shopping spree of my dreams."

She laughed. The man was full of surprises—she'd give him that. Her gaze fell to his lips again. Lord, she really liked those lips. But he was off-limits. Period. Amen.

Carmen sighed and stared out the window instead. "Sorry. No credit card. And don't expect me to climb a balcony for you either. When we part ways, I'll let you go for good."

"We'll see…" He winked, then closed his eyes again, apparently continuing his nap.

Carmen leaned her head back against the chair and did the same, though sleep evaded her. Instead her mind churned with thoughts of them getting caught and her new career and the new future she'd planned in a shambles around her.

No. She jolted awake. Time to shape up and concentrate on her goals. Get to the resort, get through her final interviews, get the job. Nothing else mattered. Not her feelings, not the hot guy beside her, not the incredible chemistry between them.

Nothing.

No matter how she might long for a real partner to share her life with someday…

CHAPTER FOUR

HALF AN HOUR later Zac sat beside Carmen in the limo they were sharing with Priya and Lance, zooming down the road. They crested a ridge and the Arctic Star Resort was still a sight to behold, even after all these years.

Zac battled a tingle of adrenaline, seeing the towering pine and glass entryway of the main lodge, and instead focused on the glow of lights from the smaller though no less impressive private chalets in the far distance, across an open plain.

That was where he'd lived, growing up.

Memories of happier times, of coming home to the wonderful smells of his mother's cooking, game nights, laughter and hugs and comfort and peace assaulted him before he shoved them away. Those days were over and best left forgotten.

Their driver pulled up under the massive portico at the front of the lodge and Zac helped Car-

men out of one side of the vehicle while Lance
did the same with Priya on the other. Thankfully their traveling companions had been too
busy chattering about the upcoming conference
and the scenery to start another round of Twenty
Questions, but Zac still felt on edge.

He made an excuse to stay by the limo and
make sure the bellman got all the luggage, but
really he just needed a moment alone before
walking into what he considered a war zone.

His father had built this resort from the
ground up, after making a name for himself by
running several large luxury hotels throughout
the world. Taking his years of knowledge with
him after breaking out on his own nearly thirty
years ago, Jonathan Taylor had quickly amassed
an international empire, including hotels and resorts in fourteen countries and fifteen states in
America. Thirty properties total, the last Zac
knew, and probably still growing.

His father had turned sixty the previous year,
but showed no signs of slowing down. During
his younger days Zac would've been proud of
his father's accomplishments. Now, he just felt
disappointed.

Once the luggage had been safely loaded onto
a trolley, Zac followed the bellman into the glorious lobby of the resort. High cathedral ceilings soared above them and the glow of warm

lighting glimmered off the shiny pine floors. He'd grown up here, with room service and valets and maids. He'd hung out with the cooks and the housekeepers and the security guards. They'd been like his second family.

"There you are!" Carmen linked arms with him, the copper in her curls gleaming beneath the chandeliers hanging from huge beams above. "Isn't this place gorgeous?"

He gave a curt nod. It was beautiful—but not nearly as beautiful as her.

"Wow." Priya had walked over to a round marble table near the center of the lobby. In the middle of it sat an enormous cut-crystal vase, brimming with white lilies and roses. She leaned in to sniff a bloom, then squinted at the vase. "That's Waterford. Worth thousands of dollars."

She was correct. Zac's father spared no expense when it came to the décor in his hotels.

"Smile, please," Carmen whispered.

Her warm breath sent a shiver of awareness through him, bringing him back to the present.

"We're supposed to be happy and in love."

It seemed keeping up a happy façade would be more difficult than he'd anticipated.

"Priya…" Lance said, plopping down on one of the overstuffed suede sofas that Zac knew were handmade in London. "These chairs are amazing. We should get a couple of these for our apartment."

"They wouldn't fit through the door," Priya said, snuggling up beside him. "Too big."

"C'mon, let's get checked in." Zac steered Carmen toward the reservation desk. Lance and Priya followed.

"Miss Sanchez?" A woman stepped out from behind the nearby concierge desk and walked over to meet them. "Welcome to the Arctic Star Resort and Spa. My name is Willow. And this must be Miss Shaw."

The woman shook their hands, then handed them gift bags emblazoned with the logo of the California clinic on the side.

"We're so happy to have you here. Please follow me. I've taken the liberty of booking each of you into your suites already, and the bellman has been instructed to deliver your luggage as we speak. I'll show you to your rooms. Please do let me know if there's anything you need during your stay. Miss Sanchez, you and your guest will be in the Yupik Suite. And Miss Shaw, you and your guest will be in the Aleut Suite."

They climbed a grand curving staircase to the second floor. From memory, Zac knew the wings of the hotel formed a huge square, five floors high, and surrounded a spacious courtyard in the middle, filled with flowers and blooming trees in the spring. He'd used to love playing out there as a kid. There was also a reserve near the back of the resort where the conservationists his father kept on staff cared for injured wildlife.

The group stopped to wait for the elevators to take them up to their rooms. Zac knew there were only four suites on the top floor, all named for indigenous Alaskan tribes.

Minutes later, much to Zac's relief, the concierge led Zac and Carmen to the outside door of their suite.

"Thank you, Willow," Carmen said.

"My pleasure." The concierge opened the door for them, then handed them each a keycard. "As I said, please call me if you need anything during your stay. You can reach me through the front desk from eight a.m. through eight p.m. Your evening concierge will be Dustin, and he can be reached through the front desk as well. Enjoy your stay."

"We'll talk later," Lance called as Willow led him and Priya away toward their own suite down the hall.

That was what Zac was dreading.

He held the door for Carmen, then followed her inside. The owners of the California clinic had added a few special touches to the suite, like a bottle of champagne on ice on the coffee table in the living room, and a plate of fresh strawberries covered in chocolate in the kitchenette.

The design of the suite was just as spectacular as the rest of the resort. High ceilings, huge windows overlooking the beautiful landscape, all the furniture plush and inviting. There was a large living room, a dining area with a table that seated eight, and a kitchenette with stove, fridge, and granite countertops.

He and Carmen went down a short hallway to the master suite, with an enormous king-sized bed in the center of the room, a sitting area with a love seat, chairs and table near the windows, a walk-in closet, and a private balcony with a small table and chairs outside as well. The master bath was as big as the bedroom, complete with double vanities, a whirlpool tub and an entire wall of mirrors, along with a gigantic walk-in glass shower.

If it had been anywhere but his father's resort, Zac could've happily stayed there indefinitely. As it was, he couldn't wait to get back to his small, comfy apartment back in Anchorage. His EMT salary wasn't huge, but it covered his bills, plus a few splurges. He'd walked away from his inheritance when he'd severed all ties to his family and he didn't miss it. Not too much, anyway.

They went back into the bedroom and found their luggage sitting neatly stacked atop the racks in the corner. The items he'd had delivered earlier—his tux and some additional shirts and suits—had been pressed and hung in the walk-in closet.

Money didn't buy happiness, but it did make life a bit easier sometimes.

"You're awfully quiet again." Carmen sat atop the bed, the expensive Egyptian cotton sheets rustling beneath her. "Having second thoughts?"

"No." Zac unzipped his bag. "Just tired."

"Hmm…" Carmen took off her boots, then removed her parka. "The welcome reception is at seven, which leaves us about three hours to kill."

"Good. I could use some time to relax and recharge before we deal with Lance and Priya again."

He headed for the dresser with an armload of socks and briefs, only to collide with Carmen halfway there.

"Sorry."

"My fault."

She stepped back slightly, but not before her heat penetrated his cotton shirt. Her breath caught and her wide eyes met his. Gauging her reaction, he saw he wasn't the only one feeling that flare of desire between them once more.

The best thing to do would be to walk away, but he couldn't seem to get his feet to move.

"No problem."

His words emerged huskier than usual, and his gaze flickered to the bed before he could stop himself. He leaned in slightly, closing the distance between them. She was so close, so soft, so tempting… That was when he stopped. She also looked so…*nervous*.

Zac frowned and straightened. "Everything okay?"

Carmen nodded and held her hand over her heart.

Out of habit, Zac set his things aside, then took her wrist and checked her pulse—it was hard and fast.

"Listen, I would never force you to do anything you don't want—"

"I know that. It's fine. I just…" She exhaled and looked up at him. "My stomach's bothering me, that's all."

"You're not getting sick, are you?" He tilted his head slightly, concerned, and then felt her forehead. "I've got my EMT pack with me. Had it sent with my other stuff. I can get a thermometer and check if you give me a minute."

"No. I'm fine. It's just stress. With the conference and the job and this pretend engagement. Which is silly, right? I mean it was *my* idea, but now it seems a lot harder than I expected, and awkward, and…"

"No. It's not silly at all."

She was babbling—something he knew she did when she got flustered. Normally he found it endearing. But the fact it was happening now had his pulse speeding up too, with adrenaline and anticipation.

He tugged gently on her wrist, bringing her closer. "I know how you can get."

"It's crazy. I know," Carmen said. "I'm always cool, calm and collected. I shouldn't let any of this get to me. It's all pretend. It doesn't mean anything. It isn't—"

"Shh…" Zac placed a finger over her lips. "Just breathe. No pressure. Think of this as us just hanging out with the gang after work. Maybe we're at the Snaggle Tooth, having drinks after a shift. Talking, laughing, relaxing. Wendy's doing awful karaoke with Tom. Jake and Molly have the twins. It's all cool. No big deal at all…"

She nodded, inhaling deeply, her gaze locked with his.

"Good." He rubbed his thumb back and forth over the underside of the wrist to calm her pulse. "You are going to be great this weekend. You're smart and funny and the best damned midwife I've ever met." He smiled. "You've got this."

Carmen gave him another nod, her pulse slowing at last.

"That's it. Good. Relax and enjoy the weekend."

She exhaled slowly, her cheeks flushing a pretty shade of pink. "You're right. I got this."

"Yes, you do." He let her go before he couldn't, and reached for his stuff on top of the dresser. "Now, go have a nice hot bath to take the edge off. We'll talk some more when you're done."

A short while later Carmen sat in the tub with bubbles up to her neck, doing her best to forget the connection sizzling between her and Zac and failing miserably.

But indulging in fantasies about the man and their one night together was pointless. They wouldn't be repeating that here. She'd made her rules for a reason and it was high time she stuck to them.

Rules were what she lived by. Rules kept her safe.

Leaving things until the last minute and being spontaneous wasn't her thing. She liked her life all planned out.

Back in Trinidad, she'd made budgets and schedules to keep track of everything for their household, ensuring they had enough money to last each month. When she'd been in nursing school her organization skills had come in handy as well, juggling classes and jobs and internships.

Unfortunately those skills didn't translate well to love and emotion.

She'd tried to plan out her relationship with Steve, but he'd claimed she was too cold and calculating, always leading with her brain and not her heart.

The one time she'd tried leading with her heart had been the night of that party, with Zac, and, well...those results weren't exactly stellar. So, yeah. Maybe she should've just been up-front with the owners of the California clinic and told them the truth instead of a bunch of lies.

It was all just so stressful and sordid and screwed up.

Ugh.

She reached over and hit the little button on the side of the tub to turn on the jets, then closed her eyes to shut out the world. The water hit her in all the right spots, easing the knots in the muscles of her back and shoulder blades and lulling her into a kind of half sleep.

She pictured Zac in the bedroom, standing so close to her she could see the tiny flecks of gold in his eyes, see the shadow of stubble on his jaw, hear the sharp intake of his breath as he leaned in.

Warmth spread outward from her core and moisture gathered between her legs. It had nothing to do with the bath water. She imagined his strong, capable hands taking the place of those jets. Pressure inside her built as memories of the two of them together in bed flashed into her mind. The heat of his skin beneath her fingertips, the hardness of his muscles pressed against her soft curves, the sound of his deep groans as he'd reached his ultimate pleasure…

Buzz, buzz, buzz…

The sound of her cell phone vibrating on the vanity jarred her back to reality. She shut off the jets, then quickly stood to grab a towel and wrap it around herself. Thankfully she managed to catch the caller ID and answer before they hung up.

"Carmen Sanchez," she said, taking a seat on the edge of the tub as it drained.

While the labor and delivery nurse from Anchorage Mercy on the other end of the line went over some new complications with one of her patients, Carmen pulled on a robe from the back of the door, then walked out of the bathroom—where she found Zac lying on the bed, his shirt and shoes off. Her mouth went dry as she stopped in the doorway, staring at his sculpted, toned torso.

Distracted, she lost track of the conversation on her phone. "I'm sorry. Could you repeat that, please?"

Zac looked up from the guest directory he was reading and narrowed his gaze. "Work?"

She nodded, her wicked thoughts in the tub flooding her brain again as she stared at his sleek, chiseled perfection. His dark skin glowed beneath the bedside lamp and she clenched her hand tight around the phone to keep herself from reaching for him.

"Nurse Davis? Hang on a moment, please. I need to write this down."

She covered the phone with one hand and hurried down the hall toward the front of the suite, praying Zac wouldn't follow. Because if he came after her now she wasn't sure she'd be able to resist, and resist she must. There was too much riding on this weekend to screw it up with sex and messy emotion.

Alone, Zac sank back down onto the end of the bed and scrubbed his hands over his head. What the hell had he been thinking, lounging around waiting for her to come out of the bathroom? This wasn't a couple's getaway. They were here to work. She was here to win the job of her dreams and he was here as her fake fiancé.

Still, when she'd come out in nothing but that robe, her mocha skin dewy and pink from her bath, her pretty eyes widening as she looked at him, he'd gotten so caught up in the moment it had been easy to forget all that other stuff.

Maybe it was the prospect of being stuck here in this suite with her for the next couple of days that made him start thinking about all the places on her he'd like to lick and suck. Places he remembered from their one-night stand that he definitely wouldn't mind revisiting—her lovely breasts, that spot just below her belly button that made her squirm if he teased it just right with his tongue…

Dammit.

This was ridiculous. He was a grown man—not some randy teenager.

Frustrated, he pushed to his feet and grabbed the resort directory again. There was plenty to do around here to keep him busy. It seemed his father had made plenty of upgrades in the twelve years since Zac had been gone. And if he didn't want to go out he could watch TV, order an in-room massage, check his emails and surf the internet…

Except none of those ideas appealed to him. He felt too restless to stay cooped up in here—

especially with Carmen just down the hall in nothing but a robe. Besides, he wasn't one to sit around and wait. He liked *doing* things, being active.

That was why his career as an EMT suited him so well. Even when they didn't have a call he could restock the truck, take inventory, prep gear and equipment. Plus, there were always other people around. Zac didn't like to be alone. It allowed him to get in his own head too much, think about the past.

Decision made, Zac changed into jeans and a T-shirt, then pulled on socks and shoes before waving to Carmen as he passed and heading out of the room. Hoping to burn off some excess energy, he took the stairwell across the hall from the room and headed down to the lobby.

The first floor was as busy as ever when he arrived, filled with guests for the conference. That was good, because he didn't want to risk being recognized. He stuck to the outskirts of the room as he made his way over to the concierge's desk, scanning the crowds constantly for any sign of his parents, but thankfully finding none.

His father had used to be present for all major events at this resort, but perhaps that had changed. He probably had many more important jobs to do in his other hotels.

"How is your room, sir?" Willow asked as he approached the desk. "Anything I can assist you with?"

"Everything's great. Thanks." He glanced around him, then lowered his voice. "The other concierge you mentioned earlier—the one who works at night? Dustin? His last name doesn't happen to be Lewis, does it?"

She smiled. "It does. Do you know him?"

"Maybe."

Zac released a pent-up breath. Dustin Lewis had been a good friend to him during his teens and he felt like the only person here he could trust now.

"You said he comes on duty at eight?"

"Yes, sir. But he's usually here early. Likes to socialize with the other staff before his shift." Willow chuckled. "Shall I page him for you?"

"No, no. That's fine." Zac looked around again. "If you tell me where he might be I can find him myself. Thanks."

"Try by the pool. He likes to sit out there and watch the sunset." Willow pointed to a hallway on the right. "Last door at the end."

"Great."

He headed out through the controlled chaos of the lobby and down a quieter corridor to the glass door at the end. The smell of chlorine stirred more memories of his childhood here.

He'd learned to swim in this pool with his parents. His dad had taught him how to dive. He still remembered the joy on his father's face when he'd completed his first lap in under two minutes.

Good times. Until everything had gone bad.

Zac pulled open the door and walked into the heated glass atrium covering the Olympic-sized swimming pool. The air was more humid here, and his sinuses opened up as he took a deep breath.

Sure enough, he located Dustin on one of the lounge chairs on the far side of the otherwise deserted pool, staring out at the sky in the distance. It was still early, not even five yet, but this far north evening came early in March.

Not wanting to startle the older man, he stopped a short distance away and cleared his throat. "Been a while, Dustin."

"What the...?" Dustin sat forward and slowly turned, his grin widening. "Zachary Taylor—get over here and give me a hug, boy. Where have you been keeping yourself?"

Zac embraced his friend, then took a seat on the edge of the chaise across from Dustin's. "I live in Anchorage now. Work as a paramedic."

"A paramedic? I always knew you were smart." Dustin nodded, his smile fading as his expression turned serious. "Your father know you're here?"

"No." Zac hung his head and rubbed his hand over the back of his neck. "And I'd prefer to keep it that way. Please don't say anything to him about seeing me, okay?"

"Your secret's safe with me. Besides, they don't live on this property anymore. Moved to that new place he bought in Chicago about a year ago. They stay in the penthouse suite there, from what I understand," Dustin said, narrowing his gaze on Zac as his smile returned. "So, tell me about yourself. You married? Got kids?"

"Neither." Zac's mind was still churning over the news that he might make it through this weekend without having to encounter his parents at all. He needed to make certain, though.

"Hmm…" The older man nodded slightly. "Too bad. About the kids, I mean. Always thought you'd make a great dad."

"Given the role model I had, I doubt it." Zac shrugged and peered at the darkening sky, at the streaks of gold and purple and bright red-orange fading into indigo. "How about you? How's Martha?"

A shadow of sadness passed over the older man's face. "My Martha passed away last year. Stroke. Took her fast, so for that I'm grateful."

"I'm so sorry." Zac reached over to place his hand on Dustin's shoulder. "I didn't know."

"How could you? You weren't here." Dustin exhaled slowly. "Anyway, kids and grandkids are doing well. Added another to the fold back in January. Little girl named Zoey."

"Congratulations." Zac waited while his friend brought up some pictures on his phone to show him. "Wow, she's beautiful. She's got your eyes."

"Yeah. Got my lungs too. Cries loud enough sometimes to be heard clear over in Siberia."

Zac chuckled. "Nice! Man, I miss seeing you around every day."

"Maybe you should come back more often, then."

Dustin clicked off his phone and shoved it in his pocket. That was when Zac noticed the white gauze wrapped around the older man's wrist, peeking out from beneath the cuff of his uniform dress shirt.

"Hurt yourself?" Zac asked.

"Huh?" Dustin frowned, then glanced at the bandage. "Oh, this. It's nothing. Cut myself on a knife making dinner the other day. No big deal."

From the dried blood stain on the gauze, it looked like some kind of a deal to Zac. "How's your diabetes?" he asked.

Dustin gave a dismissive wave. "Fine, fine... You trying to be my doctor now, boy?"

"No." Zac had caught the irritation in the older man's voice and he decided to keep the peace and let the matter drop—after one last thing. "But I *am* a trained medical caregiver. I'm just concerned about you, that's all. If you want me to take a look at that cut, let me know. Things heal slower because of your diabetes, remember?"

"I do. And I'm perfectly capable of taking care of myself. Been doing it long enough."

Zac shook his head and chuckled, leaning back in his chair to gaze out the window as Dustin had been doing before. The sun had set now, and the first few stars were glimmering.

I'm perfectly capable of taking care of myself...

The fact that Carmen had said nearly those exact words to him wasn't lost on him. Neither was the fact that he needed to get back to the suite and get changed for the welcome reception soon.

"So, my parents aren't here at all this weekend, then?"

"Didn't say that. Only that they don't live here permanently anymore." Dustin reclined again in his own lounge chair and gave Zac a sideglance. "You know how your father is—doesn't like to leave anything to chance. With that big conference here this weekend, I wouldn't be surprised at all if he flies in for at least part of it. Why'd you come back, though, if not to see him and make amends? Your mother misses you terribly. Never talks about it, but I can tell."

Zac's heart nosedived a little at that. He missed his mother too. "I'm helping out a friend."

"Hmm... You always were thinking of others." Dustin shrugged. "Well, if you're trying to avoid your dad, I'd keep an eye out. Don't know his schedule, but he likes to lurk at big events."

Hopefully, with all the other attendees at the conference, he and Carmen would be able to blend into the crowd.

"How is she?" he asked.

"Your mother? Fine. They're both fine, far as I can tell. Not much changes around here, Zac—you know that." Dustin pointed out the window. "Same mountains, same snow, same glorious landscape. It's what I love about the place. Comforting to think that all places remain, regardless of what we do, constant and unchanging. Helps me not feel so lonely."

"Yeah..." Zac said, feeling a similar pang of yearning inside himself.

His self-reliance might come in handy on the job, but in his personal life it tended to isolate him. Hook-ups were easy to come by. Real intimacy that required trust and true vulnerability…? Not so much.

"Look, boy. Is this still about what happened with your father all those years ago? I know you were disappointed in him when he ran around with that other woman. I get it. I do. He's your dad. You idolized him. He made a mistake. But then we all have. He's human, Zac. Just like me. Just like you. Maybe you should—"

"I need to go."

Zac pushed to his feet, frowning down at Dustin. He loved his old friend, but the last thing he needed right now was a lecture on forgiving his father's past sins.

"I've got a reception tonight to get ready for."

"I'll come with you," Dustin said, getting up himself, ignoring Zac's offer of help.

Back in the day, the older man had used to tower over Zac. Now they were the same height, Dustin's proud shoulders bent by age.

"My shift starts soon," he said.

They walked back toward the entrance to the pool. Thankfully, Dustin let the matter of Zac's relationship with his dad drop. He held the door for Dustin, then followed him out into the hallway.

"If you change your mind about that cut, my friend and I are staying in the Yupik Suite.

Come up anytime and I'll clean and dress it for you."

"Will do." Dustin shuffled along beside him on the plush carpeted floor. "And don't be a stranger this weekend. If you do run into your father let those old wounds heal, son. Life's too short. My Martha taught me that."

"Some wounds are too deep to heal," Zac said, stopping outside the door to the stairwell.

"Perhaps we just don't give them enough of a chance to get better. Things aren't always what they seem. Remember that. Nobody's perfect. Not even you, boy."

The older man looked at him a moment, before continuing on down the hall toward the lobby, speaking to Zac over his shoulder.

"See you around. Try and stay out of trouble while you're here."

"No point," he said, more to himself than anyone else, and then headed back to the room.

The truth was, Zac knew trouble had already come, right in the minute he'd agreed to come on this trip with Carmen. In hindsight, it would've been wiser to say no. But then he'd not exactly been thinking with the correct part of his anatomy when she'd asked him. Come to think of it, that happened most times when she was around.

Now they were here, and he was in too far to get out.

All he could do was keep moving forward until the weekend was done.

CHAPTER FIVE

ELLEN LANDON, SIXTY years old and the owner of the clinic in Big Sur, California, sat between Carmen and Priya at the welcome reception that night at their table for six.

Carmen had only seen photos of the woman online, and she'd always reminded her of a stately Dame Judi Dench. Despite approaching what some would consider retirement age, Ellen Landon showed no signs of slowing down. She kept as active and vibrant as many people twenty years younger, and showed no signs of selling her practice anytime soon.

Across from Ellen at the white-linen-covered table, between Zac and Lance, was Ellen's wife—an OB-GYN physician named Elizabeth Nguyen. Their progressive practice had helped pave the way for the future of midwifery in the state of California.

To work with two such pioneers in the field would be an honor—not to mention that mentorship from Ellen and her team alone would be worth more than gold. Of course the bump in pay and the promotion to clinic supervisor would be nice as well…

"I'm so glad you both made it to the conference," Ellen said, smiling at Carmen and Priya in turn on either side of her. "And it's so nice to meet your significant others as well. How long have you and your fiancé been dating, Carmen?"

"Not long, Ms. Landon," Carmen said, avoiding Priya's hawklike gaze from the other side of Ellen. "We've been seeing each other for a few months."

"Yes, it happened *so* fast," Priya said, narrowing her gaze on Carmen. "Took us all by surprise."

"Sure did," Lance said from across the table, elbowing Zac in the arm. "Man, if I'd known you two were hot and heavy after the Christmas party I would've been all over that."

"That's exactly why we didn't tell you," Zac said, giving his friend a flat stare.

"That's wonderful. I do love a whirlwind romance. And, please, call me Ellen," the older woman said, seemingly oblivious to the tension around the table. "Congratulations on your engagement, Carmen. Such an exciting time in life. I remember when Liz and I were planning our wedding. So much to do…so little time. And you, Priya. How long have you and Lance been together?"

"Almost a year." Priya kept her gaze steady on Carmen. "We're taking our time with things— not rushing. I prefer to plan, so I don't miss anything important. It must be hard for you, Carmen, having it sprung on you like that. I always thought we were alike when it came to organization. I mean, there's so much to do… so many details."

Forcing the knots in her stomach to ease, Carmen plastered on her best smile. "Yes, you're right. I do like to plan everything out. But love is what it is."

"Hmm…" Suspicion gleamed in Priya's dark eyes. "What date have you set for the wedding?"

"Oh, we haven't really gotten that far yet. Just enjoying the moment for now."

"Sure…" Priya sounded completely unconvinced. She exchanged a quick glance with Lance, then looked back at Carmen. "What about a dress? Flowers? Venue? You should start planning all that before you even set a date. What's Zac's favorite color?"

Carmen's mind raced through the facts on the sheet he'd given her. "Blue."

"Favorite food?"

"Anything Mexican."

"Favorite movie?"

"*Die Hard.*"

Carmen's stomach clenched. This was worse than the lightning round on her mother's favorite TV game show. She swallowed hard against the lump of stress in her throat. Beneath the table Zac took her hand for moral support.

"What does his favorite movie have to do with our wedding?"

"Nothing," Priya said, giving her a sly smile. "Just asking."

"How are the suites?"

Ellen switched subject and Carmen couldn't have been more relieved.

"Ours is beautiful."

"Our room is gorgeous, thanks. This whole resort is amazing—don't you think, *doux-doux*?" Carmen gave Zac's hand a squeeze.

"Yes, gorgeous," Zac said, his gaze locked on her. "Very lovely indeed."

A fresh wave of heat danced over her skin, this time nothing to do with embarrassment and everything to do with the man beside her— which was bad. Very, very bad.

She was here to impress Ellen Landon, not to flirt with Zac.

"Mr. Taylor?" Ellen said. "You're a paramedic?"

"Yes, ma'am." He sipped his Scotch. "Best EMT in Anchorage. And please call me Zac."

"Zac, then." The older woman nodded. "I bet you could swap some stories with my wife. She's always telling me horror stories from her shifts in the ER."

"I'm sure I could," he said, shifting his attention to Liz. "Do you work at a large facility?"

Grateful to have the spotlight off her, Carmen took a deep breath and smoothed her hand down the front of her simple black dress. It was far from revealing, even with its thin straps that left her shoulders bare. But with the sizzling looks Zac kept giving her tonight she felt as if he could see right through it.

Talk about making a girl feel like the belle of the ball.

She tried not to read too much into it, though. He was probably just pulling from his usual bag of tricks to get through this weekend.

Thankfully, a server arrived with the first course of their catered gourmet meal—zucchini carpaccio with salt-broiled shrimp—and saved her from a further round of Twenty Questions from Priya.

As they ate, Ellen turned the conversation to business.

"Both your résumés are quite accomplished and interesting," Ellen said. "But it was the presentations each of you submitted for the direction you'd like to take the clinic in for the future that I found most intriguing." She ate a bite of her salad before continuing. "They were the reason each of you were chosen as finalists for the position. In the end, however, there's only one position available. It's all we can allow for in the budget right now. So I'd like you each to talk more about your plans for the training program. Priya, why don't you start?"

"My concentration would be on preventing gestational diabetes and hyperactive disorders with screening and integrative management in early pregnancy. In my experience, the pathogenesis of these conditions is multifactorial, and includes lifestyle factors such as nutrition, stress level and stress management resources, and physical activity…"

As her colleague discussed her ideas for the new California clinic, Carmen nibbled on her salad. She'd barely taken more than a few bites, though, before Zac shifted in his seat and his thigh brushed against hers. Zings of fresh electricity jolted through her system and memories of them in the suite after her bath, with her in just a robe and him naked from the waist up, filled her head before she could stop them.

"And you, Carmen?" Ellen asked. "Can you talk about your training plans, please?"

Focus, girl. Focus.

"Sure, yes," Carmen said.

She gave herself a firm mental warning to stay out of Smutty Land where Zac was concerned. It was time to dazzle with her amazing midwifery ideas, not dream about tackling Zac into bed and having her wicked way with him.

"My main focus would be on providing a framework to assist midwives in developing a consistent approach to screening for perinatal mood and anxiety disorders. I'd like to develop brief interventions and strategies for referral, response to emergent situations, and a follow-up to ensure continuity of care."

"Both of those ideas are excellent," Ellen said. "My plan is to have whoever takes over the management of the midwife staff at the clinic helping to design and implement the new training courses *you* discussed, Carmen, and also to develop an innovative screening and prevention planning program aiming to reduce the incidence and severity of the conditions *you* mentioned, Priya."

"I've been reading up on those conditions myself," Carmen said, congratulating herself on sounding competent and professional, instead of showing the mass of quivering nerves she felt inside.

She didn't even feel bad about elbowing her way into Priya's topic. This was, after all, a competition—even if they were friends. She wanted to show Ellen that by hiring her she'd get someone knowledgeable on both topics.

"The articles I've read suggest including standardized screenings and prevention programs based on a patient's risk level, then incorporating medical management, education and lifestyle interventions. Through my own research I've identified at least three evidence-based prevention strategies for lowering patient risk of gestational diabetes and/or hypertensive disorders. I look forward to presenting you both with a detailed, comprehensive outline at my final interview."

Not to be outshone, Priya launched into a spiel on midwife management of pelvic organ prolapse across a patient's lifespan. By the time she'd finished, their main course had arrived— braised pork with pearl onions and grapes.

Zac was being Mr. Charming, as usual, and even if the rest of the weekend went to hell in a handbasket Carmen knew that at least she'd gotten the best out of him in the schmoozing department. Every once in a while, though, she caught him scanning the crowd, as if looking for someone. Which was odd, since neither of them had been to the resort before.

Then she remembered Lance mentioning Zac had been off his game recently and that he wasn't seeing anyone at present. Was he looking to hook up with someone here? The man was drop-dead gorgeous, and smart and funny, and any woman would be lucky to have him, and…

Ugh.

Thinking about that would get her nowhere but depressed. Which was silly, because she and Zac weren't really a couple. She had no right to be jealous of him seeing other people—even if he was supposed to pretend to be hers for the weekend.

So why does the idea of him fawning over someone else bug me so much?

Maybe because, deep down, she wanted to find someone who'd fawn over *her* that way?

Dessert was served at last—slices of hazelnut-and-chocolate meringue cake—and a small band in the corner began to play. Several couples from the surrounding tables headed for the dance floor in front of the stage, and Zac held his hand out to her.

"Carmen, dance with me."

She excused herself and let him lead her to the dance floor. He took her in his arms once they found an open spot amongst the other couples swaying to the music. It all seemed a bit surreal—him looking like he'd just stepped off the cover of a magazine in his fancy tuxedo instead of the bland EMT uniform he usually wore for work.

Then he pulled her closer and his scent surrounded her—soap, sandalwood, and a hint of vanilla. *Delicious.* Her first instinct was to bury her face in the side of his neck and inhale deeply. Then she remembered where they were, and who they were, and remained a respectable distance away.

"Dinner went pretty well, I think," he said against her temple.

"Yes. Thank goodness for those dossiers."

"Right… Even if mine *was* on the skimpy side."

His legs brushed against hers and the simmering attraction inside her boiled higher.

"I memorized yours, just in case," he said.

She laughed. "Okay. When's my birthday?"

"August twelfth."

"Favorite song?"

He tilted his head slightly and smiled. "This one, as a matter of fact. 'The Way You Look Tonight.' Though you prefer the Michael Bublé version. Why do you think I asked you to dance?"

"Smooth." She rested her forehead against his chest so he wouldn't see how much he'd touched her heart. "Favorite color?"

"Purple. Lavender, to be exact."

"Middle name?"

"Ramona. After your mother."

"Wow. You *are* good."

"That's what all the ladies say," he joked.

She leaned back and smacked his arm. "Thanks for the reminder."

That was when she noticed him nodding to an elderly African-American gentleman with white hair, standing near the service entrance.

"Who is that?" Carmen asked, curious.

"Dustin—the night concierge. I met him earlier, while you were running around the resort in your robe."

"I was not running around in my robe." Carmen gave him a look, biting back a smile at the teasing look in his eyes, happier than she cared to admit about having his full attention back on her. "I had to deal with that call about my patient. Everything's fine there, by the way."

"Never doubted it for a minute."

He chuckled, the deep, rich sound reverberating through her like honey.

"Even if you *were* working in your robe."

"What is it with you and my robe?" She shook her head and grinned. "What difference does it make anyway? They couldn't see me. As long as the patient was treated properly, that's all that matters."

"Hmm..." He steered them into a quieter corner of the dance floor and bent slightly to put his mouth near her ear. "Well, all I can say is

I'm glad none of the other men from Anchorage Mercy can see you here tonight. Because you're beautiful, Carmen, and I don't want to share."

Zac held Carmen closer than was probably wise as they swayed to the music in the shadows, deep in the crowd and yet far away from the prying eyes of the rest of their table.

Honestly, at that moment Carmen could have got any man to do whatever she wanted. That dress of hers should be illegal in all fifty states. The black silky material clung to her curves enough to hint at the glory beneath without giving anything away. Tiny straps over her shoulders led to a V-shaped neckline that revealed just a tantalizing hint of her perfect cleavage. The skirt fell to mid-thigh, showing enough shapely leg to make him picture everything underneath.

She wore her hair up tonight, although a few of her curls had managed to escape and dangle around her face and throat, and her remarkable green-gold eyes sparkled with intelligence and determination. She was a woman to be reckoned with, and so lovely it almost hurt to look at her.

"Have I told you how beautiful you look tonight?"

"You did—thank you." She beamed up at him

and smoothed her hand down his tux-covered chest. "You look pretty spectacular yourself."

He smiled. This felt good—right—being here with her like this. If things had been different— if he'd been a different man, a better man—he'd have asked her to be his, and not just for the weekend either. But he was who he was, and he had a past she knew nothing about.

He managed to mumble, "Thanks."

The band finished the song and began another—one of his favorites this time. "Unforgettable" by Nat King Cole. He kept reminding himself that this was all for show, but it was getting harder to remember as they rocked gently on the dance floor. He couldn't help pulling her a bit closer, until she rested her head on his chest and the sweet jasmine fragrance of her hair tickled his nose.

"I like dancing with you," he said. Lame, considering he'd like to do a lot more than just dance with her, but it would have to do.

"I like dancing with you too," she whispered. "This is nice."

"Nice" didn't begin to cover what he felt, holding her in his arms. He wanted to pick her up and carry her back to their room, make love to her all night long, but unfortunately after the song ended, reality returned. The couples around them began to leave the dance floor and

Zac forced himself to step back, away from temptation.

"We should…uh…probably get back to the table, so you can dazzle your new bosses some more."

Carmen sighed and nodded, frowning down at her shoes. "Yes, we probably should."

By the time they weaved their way back to the table it was just Ellen and Liz there, discussing their favorite vacation spots around the world. Growing up, Zac had traveled extensively with his father, to visit all of his hotel and resort holdings. He'd never thought it would come in handy, but if it helped win Carmen her dream job he'd add what he could to the conversation.

"Where are Priya and Lance?" Carmen asked as she took her seat.

"Oh, Priya wasn't feeling well all of a sudden," Ellen said. "Lance took her to the restroom. I do hope she's all right."

"Maybe I should go check on her," Carmen said.

Before she could get up, however, Lance and Priya returned, to take their seats once more. Priya looked a little pale, and Lance didn't appear much better.

"Everything all right?" Carmen asked.

"Yes, fine. Thanks." Priya kept ahold of Lance's hand. "What are we discussing?"

"Vacation destinations," Liz said.

"Awesome," Lance said. "Anyone ever been to Italy?"

"I have," Zac said. "Florence is one of my favorite places on earth—other than Barcelona."

"What about you, Carmen?" Priya asked. "Travel much?"

"Not really. Unless you count moving my family here from Trinidad after nursing school," she said, crossing her legs toward Zac and giving him another glimpse of those gorgeous legs. "I was always too busy working to go on vacation."

"Well, maybe you can plan a nice trip for your honeymoon," Ellen suggested. "Liz and I went to South America on ours. Rio, Costa Rica, Belize… Beautiful area."

"Yes, that would be nice," Carmen said. She exchanged a glance with Zac.

A buzz of conversation had started near the entrance to the banquet room and suddenly Zac caught sight of his parents entering. *Damn.* Time to leave.

He stood and helped a surprised Carmen to her feet. "We should go back to our room," he said, pushing to his feet. "Early start for you tomorrow. You need to get your rest. Ellen and Liz—it was a pleasure meeting you both, and thank you so much for everything this weekend."

Ellen stood as well and shook his hand. "Glad you're enjoying it, Zac. Be sure to take advantage of some of the amenities while you're here, since we'll be keeping Carmen busy for the next few days."

"I'll do that. I wouldn't want to distract her with such an important job on the line." Zac flashed them his most charming smile and then he slipped his arm around Carmen's shoulders and tugged her into his side, kissing the top of her head while keeping an eye on the exit. "Ready, darling?"

Carmen gave him a confused look. "What's going—"

He kissed her soundly, cutting her off. By the time he lifted his head she was blushing, he was breathless, and everyone at the table was watching them with a knowing gleam in their eye.

"You can stay here if you want," he said at last, a bit stunned himself by the heat of their kiss. "I just really want to go back to our room."

"I bet you do," Lance whispered slyly.

Zac gave his friend a withering stare. "I'm tired."

"Sure you are." Priya shook her head and took her fiancé's hand. "I think we'll head up to *our* room too. Long day tomorrow."

"I guess we'll all make an early night of it,

then," Ellen said, putting her arm around Liz. "See you all in the morning."

"Good night," Zac said, and managed to steer Carmen out through a side entrance to the ballroom just as his parents drew too near for comfort.

With his hand on her lower back, Zac hurried Carmen toward the elevators.

"What's happening here?" she asked, after pushing the "Up" button. "You're acting strangely."

"Nothing. Nothing's wrong," he said, jamming his finger on the button himself, as if that would make it come faster.

His chest had constricted and he felt like he couldn't breathe, as if the walls were closing in, as memories of that final argument with his father flashed in his mind.

"Are you tired?" he asked.

"No, but I thought *you* were." She crossed her arms and stepped back as the elevator dinged and the doors opened. "That's why we're leaving, right?"

He exhaled slowly and boarded the elevator after her, hitting the number for their floor. "Actually, I could use some air. Maybe we could get out of here and check out some of the grounds of the resort before bed? Since you'll be cooped up indoors for the conference most of the time."

"Oh…" She fiddled with her small evening bag. "I suppose we could take a short walk."

"Great." They arrived on their floor and Zac shrugged out of his tux jacket as they walked to their room. "Let's change—then we'll go exploring."

CHAPTER SIX

CARMEN STILL WASN'T sure exactly where they were going when she came out of the bathroom a short while later, dressed in jeans and a blue turtleneck sweater. "Ready. Hope this is warm enough for where we're going."

"You're dressed fine. I thought we'd just walk around the grounds," Zac said.

He brushed her hands aside when she reached up to remove the pins from her hair. The backs of his fingers brushed the sensitive skin at the nape of her neck, and she shivered as he ran his hands through her curls.

"Blow off some steam…work off some energy. Relax…talk."

"Talk about what?" she asked as he helped her on with her coat and then shrugged into his own before taking her hand.

Normally she wasn't the best follower—especially with men who were far too charming for their own good. From the stories she'd heard, her father had been a smooth-talking playboy, and look how that had ended for her mother.

"Maybe we should just stay here and go to bed early. You're right. I do have an early start tomorrow."

He sighed and scrubbed a hand over his face, and she noticed faint lines of tension around his eyes that hadn't been there before. He looked as on edge as she'd felt at dinner. Maybe a bit of time away wouldn't hurt after all.

"Stay in the room if you want, Carmen," he said. "But I'm going. I need some air, like I said. And I thought you might enjoy some quiet time to reflect after the grilling you got at dinner tonight. Plus, we can to go over our fact sheets again—make sure we've got all the details memorized correctly in case Priya and Lance decide to quiz us again."

Maybe he was right. That interrogation at the dinner table had been pretty intense. Besides, her body was still humming with energy after dancing with him. There was no way she'd be able to sleep until she'd worked some of it off.

"Okay. Fine. Let's go."

Zac opened the door to their suite and led her out of the room. "Are you hungry?"

"We just ate."

"No. Everyone else at our table ate." They

stood before the elevator once more. "You barely touched your food. Do you skip meals a lot?"

Surprised, she blinked up at him. Most people didn't ask about her needs at all. She was there to help *them*. "No, not often. But I was nervous, meeting Ellen face-to-face for the first time. I'm surprised you noticed."

"I notice everything about you."

He gave her a toe-curling smile, raising his hand to brush an errant curl behind her ear.

"I noticed that while you picked up your wineglass a lot you only sipped from it rarely. I've noticed that you avert your gaze when you're embarrassed or ashamed—like when you mentioned the only traveling you'd done was moving your family from Trinidad to Alaska." He traced his fingertips from her ear down her cheek, then skimmed his thumb along her jawline. "That's nothing to be embarrassed about. You worked hard to get where you are."

She swallowed hard, her heart racing. "I'm not embarrassed. I just don't like talking about myself."

"Same," he murmured as the elevator bell dinged.

They rode down to the lobby, then headed outside into the brisk, clear night. The walking trails surrounding the lodge were well lit and well maintained. The snow crunched beneath her boots as they headed off into the night, with what looked like a million stars shining above them.

After about ten minutes of walking through the silent forest, where the smell of spruce was fresh in the air, Carmen couldn't contain her curiosity anymore.

She shoved her hands into the pockets of her parka for warmth, since she'd left her gloves back in the room. "You said you wanted to talk. How about telling me why you were so cagey at dinner earlier? You kept scanning the dining room like you expected your worst enemy to walk in at any moment."

He glanced over at her, frowning. "I wasn't doing that."

"Yes, you were." Carmen stepped sideways to avoid tripping over an exposed tree root, then slowed as they approached a bubbling stream partially covered with ice. "Are you sure you know where you're going? I don't want to spend the night out here, walking in circles."

"Trust me."

The certainty in his tone made her want to do just that—which only set off those warning bells in her head again.

Zac took her hand and led her a short way down to a spot where they could both jump across the water easily. Apparently he'd forgotten his gloves too, since his bare fingers were warm and steady around hers.

"It's not much farther. Over that next hill. Don't worry, I won't let you get lost in the wild tundra. An island girl like you wouldn't last an hour out here alone."

"Island girl?" She snorted. "I'm tougher than I look. Like I said, I can take care of myself, thanks. And there's nothing out here as scary as a drunk frat boy who won't take no for an answer."

Zac scowled over at her. "When did *that* happen?"

"When I was bartending at a hotel in Port of Spain. Rich college kids used to flock there in their droves during spring break. The resort had security, but sometimes they'd wait for us to get off work, thinking we were included in the free perks."

She shuddered, remembering the night one of those guys had approached her in the parking lot.

"But I took self-defense classes at my neighborhood youth center in Laventille when I was a teenager. A few well-placed elbow jabs and instep stomps do wonders to change a man's mind when he's amorous."

"I'm sorry that happened to you." He kept hold of her hand once they were across the stream. "Some men don't care about anyone but themselves."

His somber tone had her thinking that perhaps he wasn't only thinking about *her* past.

"Did you go to college?" she asked.

"University of Alaska at Anchorage."

She smiled. "That's where I got my graduate degree. What was your major?"

"I graduated in Pre-Med."

They continued up a small hill.

"You studied to be a doctor? Why did you end up as a paramedic?"

"I didn't 'end up' as a paramedic. I *chose* to be a paramedic. There's a difference."

She didn't miss the defensiveness in his voice.

"I love what I do and, like I said, I'm the best EMT in Anchorage. I love being on the front line, helping people in the worst times of their life. Having an MD after my name wouldn't change that. Do you feel 'less than' because you're a midwife and not an OB physician?"

"No, of course not." She cringed slightly. "Sorry. I didn't mean to offend you."

He sighed. "I'm sorry too. Didn't mean to snap at you."

Silence fell as they crested the top of the hill and she looked down to see rows of pens filled with animals. A couple of large buildings were outlined near the back of the area—offices, she supposed. They were dark, obviously closed this late at night. It had to be close to midnight now.

Mournful cries from the caged wolves below filled the air and Carmen swiveled toward Zac, grinning. "A zoo? In the middle of a resort?"

"Rehab center." His breath frosted on the air as he surveyed the space below them. "All the animals here are native to the area. Some have been injured and are being rehabilitated before being released back into the wild. Some of them are permanent residents, unable to be returned to nature. The keepers here use the permanent residents to teach kids in the local schools. C'mon. Let's check it out."

She followed him down the trail to the pens, amazed that he knew so much about this place. It was far enough away from the main resort that it would be hard to find by chance.

They passed enclosures holding elk and moose and reindeer. The wolves were down near the end of the row.

"Tell me how you knew this was here," she said.

"Guest directory," he said, walking over to pet the snout of a curious moose near the fencing. "Figured you might enjoy it. I love being outdoors."

"Me too." She picked up some hay from a bale nearby and held it out for one of the elks to take. "When I was back home in Trinidad I used to spend every free hour I could at the beach, watching the gulls and the dolphins and the pelicans playing offshore."

"You must miss all that warmth and sunshine this far north."

"Sometimes." She laughed as the elk nuzzled her palm, looking for more food. "But as long as my family is close—that's most important."

"Yeah…" He didn't sound convinced. "Family. What about California? If you get the job you'll be moving. Will they come with you?"

"That's the plan." Carmen glanced back at him over her shoulder. "Doesn't it bother you? Not being close with your family?"

"Not really. I miss my mother sometimes." Zac dusted his hands off on his jeans. "But it's fine. I like being independent."

"Don't you get lonely, though? Twelve years is a long time to be without family."

Taking care of her mother was difficult sometimes, with her dementia, and she and Clara sometimes fought too, but Carmen couldn't imagine living without them as a part of her life.

"Not really. I mean, that's what I have friends for, right?"

They continued on down the path through the pens, with everything quiet and peaceful around them. From the way Zac was avoiding her gaze she could tell he wanted her to drop the subject, but she just couldn't. Not yet.

"Do they live in Anchorage?"

"Who?"

"Your parents."

"No." He shrugged then shook his head. "Wouldn't matter if they did. I still wouldn't talk to my father."

She took that in for a moment, along with his troubled expression, the edge of hurt in his tone. "Well, I'm sorry for whatever happened between the two of you. What about your mother? I'm sure she misses you."

"She's the reason I left. She forgave my father for his affair. I couldn't. He broke my mother's heart. She was able to get past it, but I wasn't. To keep the peace, I left." He exhaled slowly and turned around on the path. "We should get back—it's cold out here."

Carmen trailed behind him as some things about Zac began to click into place for her. His avoidance of commitment. His fierce loyalty to his friends and his patients. His serial dating to avoid anything permanent, to avoid making the same mistakes his father had made.

Not that she felt comfortable expressing those opinions to Zac at the moment. Besides, his tone at the end had effectively slammed the door on any further conversation on the topic, which was probably for the best. Honestly, she should let it go. After this weekend they'd go their separate ways again and it wouldn't matter.

But there was something…the flicker of anger and betrayal in his eyes when he'd mentioned his father's affair.

The image he portrayed in Anchorage was always so carefree and laid-back. Now she knew it masked a deep pain and it made her feel closer to him—even closer than when they'd slept together. Because he didn't share pieces of his past often. Maybe that was why she continued to be so drawn to him. He remained an enigma, and she'd always loved solving a puzzle.

In fact, her problem-solving skills were part of the reason she was so good at her job. Putting the pieces of her patients' cases and health histories together to ensure the best outcome possible. She wondered if those same skills would work as well with Zac.

Once they'd reached the top of the hill, they stopped to look down on the animals again. A shimmer of green in the sky caught her attention. She'd seen the Northern Lights several times since moving to Anchorage, but never this vividly. Soon the entire sky was awash with hypnotic waves of greens and light blues and pinks.

"Breathtaking…" she whispered, staring up into the night sky.

"Yes, it is," he said, but he was looking at her and not at the heavenly show above them.

Time seemed to slow as Zac took Carmen in his arms, his lips brushing hers once, twice, before settling on her mouth. She gasped and he took advantage, shifting closer to deepen the kiss. He tasted of Scotch and sugar and sinful fantasy.

She'd sworn not to kiss him again, to keep things strictly platonic, but this was so perfect. *Too* perfect. His kiss was as good as she remembered, and so was the hot, solid press of him against her. She slid her fingers up his chest to twine them around his neck and a low moan escaped her throat. At the rough sound, his hands slid from her waist down to her lower back, allowing her to feel the extent of his arousal.

Heat raced through her blood despite the chilly breeze and her knees trembled. If they'd been back in their suite she'd have pushed him down on the bed and had her wicked way with him, despite her vows to the contrary. Unfortunately, they weren't in their room. They were out in the snow and the wolves were howling and her toes were numb from the cold.

Finally she forced herself to step back and gather what was left of her common sense.

They'd had a fling once. She didn't want to do that again. She had too much going on as it was. Even if Zac wanted forever this time—which he didn't—given his reputation, she wasn't interested.

Am I?

No. She was not. Because that would be stupid. Ridiculous. She knew darned well what men like Zac wanted and it wasn't commitment. Then again, *she* didn't want that either, did she? That was why she'd brought him on this trip. Their fling had been nice—hot, even—but it had been just that: a fling.

She had big things ahead of her—the possibility of this new job, goals she wanted to accomplish—and getting herself locked down into a serious relationship with a man wouldn't help her reach any of those things, would it? No, it would not. Never mind that her heart yearned for more.

So, no matter how tempting Zac and the idea of being with him permanently might be, she'd let him walk away when it was over because that was what was best for everyone.

"C'mon. Let's get back to the hotel."

Zac wasn't a stupid man. He knew as soon as Carmen ended their kiss that it was a mistake. She deserved a man who could devote himself to her one hundred percent. A man with no secrets.

That wasn't him.

Dammit.

He'd agreed to come this weekend because he'd thought it would be simple. Easy in, easy out. Easy enough to avoid his family and his past and to help her out along the way. He was finding out now that it wouldn't be.

Not that he'd come face-to-face with his father, but the man and his sins still lingered over the place and over Zac like a shroud. Carmen had been right. He *had* been on guard at dinner, waiting for an enemy—his own father. He'd managed to avoid the man for twelve years. He didn't plan to end that streak this weekend.

He knew she'd been curious about him earlier, asking all her questions. And he feared he'd been rude by not answering. But it couldn't be helped. He didn't let people close. He'd been there, done that, and had the scorch marks on his heart from getting burned by his father's deception.

Because when you let people in, allowed them into your life and your heart, you only ended up being disappointed and hurt. Never mind that he might be setting his standards too high, setting himself and everyone he cared for up to fail. He was safe, his heart was secure, and that was all that mattered. He'd made the mistake of trusting people, loving people before, with his father, and it had ripped him to shreds. So, no. He wouldn't be doing that again.

Besides, he had no business being attracted to Carmen anyway. They were friends, work colleagues. And yes, for one brilliant night they'd been lovers. But that was over. There was no point letting her in and baring his soul to her.

She was the opposite of the women he usually got involved with. She was smart. She was tough. She was proud and perfect and passionate. She'd clawed her way up from nothing to make a life for herself and her family. The thought of that frat boy attacking her back in Trinidad had him clenching his fists at his sides. If he'd been there he'd have flayed that guy alive.

But now he needed to stick to their original plan. Play his part and keep his hands to himself from here on out. He'd opened up a bit to Carmen tonight, but that would be all. It didn't matter that she was full of surprises—like the way she'd run around the hotel in nothing but a robe… Like the way she'd felt against him as they'd danced… Like the way she'd responded so passionately to his kiss.

Forget about the fact that he wanted to know what else she might do. Or say. Or if he could make her moan again like he had that night they'd spent together.

Damn.

If he wasn't careful he might lose more than his head when he was with Carmen, and that scared him most of all. Even months ago, at the party, his mind buzzing with alcohol and his blood burning with desire, he'd had an inkling that she was pretty perfect. Down-to-earth, straightforward, simple. *Real.* Everything he secretly craved.

Honestly, he was tired of superficial flings. He was tired of playing the player. He wanted more. Even though he believed deep down inside that he'd never get more. He came from bad stock. Stock that didn't measure up. Stock that couldn't be faithful if its life depended on it.

Maybe he hadn't slept with anyone since Carmen after that holiday party. And, yes, perhaps that did qualify as being monogamous. But it wasn't really a conscious choice he'd made. It was a happy accident. It didn't matter that she seemed to be the only woman he craved now. That wasn't a sign of there being something more between him and Carmen. It certainly didn't mean he'd somehow fallen for her, did it?

His heart pounded as he remembered the way his nerves had tingled from her touch, the sweet, soft sound of her moans, the dreamy glazed look in her eyes after their kiss.

Oh, God.

The realization struck him like a brick upside the head. He needed to be on guard even more this weekend. Because in some ways Carmen could hurt him far worse than his father ever had.

He cared about her—about what she thought and felt.

His father had killed any good feelings Zac had had toward him the day he'd admitted his infidelity and wounded Zac's mother to the core. Why she'd stayed married to him after that was a mystery to him, even though it had proved her loyalties to Zac.

But if she'd been willing to stay, then he'd had to go. He hadn't been able to stand to be in the same room with the man, let alone listen to more of his apologies and excuses.

He'd grown up with people constantly comparing him to his father, saying how alike they were, how they were cut from the same cloth. For years the young Zac had considered it a compliment. Hell, he'd aspired to be just like his old man. Until the day news of his father's affair had broken in the tabloids and he'd been forced to tell the truth to his wife and son.

Zac's world had gone from heaven to hell in

the span of a few hours. This man, his father, a guy he'd loved and practically worshipped, wasn't the paragon Zac had held him up to be. Turned out he was human after all—and a horrible human at that. Why else would his father have been so selfish, so deceitful, ripping his close-knit family apart and shattering the very people he'd claimed to care for most in the world?

No. Love got you nothing but pain and heartache. Best to steer well clear of all of it.

They'd reached the stream again and Zac took Carmen's hand to help her across. Her skin felt silky and smooth against his and he battled a fresh wave of desire.

But he wasn't his father. He wouldn't take what he wanted just because he could. He let her go immediately they reached the other side. And increased his pace back toward the hotel—at least until she stopped him in his tracks.

She called from behind him, "Why did you kiss me?"

Zac hesitated and closed his eyes, then swiveled to face her. "Is this a trick question?"

"No. But you're hiding something, Zac Taylor." She stood before him, gaze narrowed, as the lights from the resort glowed brighter around her. "I don't know what it is, but I'm going to find out—I promise you that. You keep too many secrets. It's not good for a man."

With that, she took off ahead of him, back up the path and into the hotel, leaving Zac to stare after her and wonder how the hell he was ever going to get out of this weekend unscathed.

CHAPTER SEVEN

BRIGHT AND EARLY the next morning, Carmen sat in her first seminar of the day, coffee in hand. The room was packed with people, including Ellen and Liz, who were sitting in the front, and Priya, who was in the chair next to Carmen's.

"Reducing cesareans is a priority for healthcare and professional organizations. And labor dystocia is the leading cause of cesareans. Delaying hospital admission until active labor is established is one evidence-based method to decrease labor dystocia diagnoses. Evidence is lacking on how best to accomplish this, but several interventions have been studied, including admission algorithms and patient and staff education. This presentation will show the results of one quality improvement project whose aim was to reduce early labor admissions and support physiologic birth through implementing evidence-based tools, and thereby decrease the nulliparous term singleton vertex cesarean rate..."

The nurse practitioner giving the talk droned on, and while Carmen found the topic interesting and informative she feared there wasn't enough caffeine in the world to keep her awake for the next two hours. After those late-night shenanigans with Zac she'd not slept well last night, tossing and turning and replaying that stupid kiss they'd shared over and over in her head.

What the hell had she been thinking, kissing him back?

It had been stupid. It had been wrong. It had been incredibly tempting.

Ugh. She had no business making out with Zac when it would never go anywhere—because it *couldn't* go anywhere. They were both established in their lives. She had her career track and he had his. Yes, they'd had sex once. Yes, it had been amazing. No, it wouldn't happen again. Even if this would be the perfect time for one last hurrah, so to speak.

You're leaving. He's available. The two of you have that whole suite to yourselves...

"So, what did you and Zac do after you left the dinner last night?" Priya whispered from beside her at the table. "Lance and I stopped by your suite, but no one answered."

"We went for a walk," Carmen said, fiddling with the notepad she'd brought with her, trying to concentrate on the speaker again. "We needed to burn off some excess energy."

"Right!" Priya chuckled. "I saw how the two of you were dancing together. I did doubt your engagement, but there's no doubting you two are hot for each other."

Heat prickled Carmen's cheeks as she scribbled unintelligible notes with her pen. "Sorry, I'm trying to hear this."

Priya gave her a side-glance and shook her head. "Right…"

"We've developed several novel tools, including an early labor triage guide, labor support checklist and early labor walking path. The triage algorithm reduced early labor admission from forty-one percent to twenty-five percent, and physiologic birth increased by two percent during the intervention. Patient experience satisfaction rates were highly positive, exceeding ninety-eight percent. The NTSV cesarean rate reduced slightly, from twenty-two percent to twenty-one percent, during this eight-week project," the presenter was saying.

Carmen did her best to catch up. And by the time she'd taken copious notes and followed along with an opportunity to explore her own clinical setting for gaps in practice and barriers to implementation, considering how to implement the new information at Anchorage Mercy, the time had passed quickly. There was a question-and-answer session at the end, followed by a break before the next session.

Priya made a beeline for Ellen and Liz, but Carmen held back a moment, wanting to collect her thoughts before approaching her potential new employers again. Besides, she needed to use the restroom.

She walked out of the bathroom to find Zac flagging her down. "Hey, what's up?" she asked as he approached.

"Do you have another seminar to get to right away?"

Carmen checked her watch. "Not for another twenty minutes. What do you need?"

"An extra set of hands." He took her by the elbow and guided her to the elevators. "I've got a friend who needs an I&D in the suite and I could use someone to help with the procedure."

"An incision and drainage?" She wrinkled her nose as the elevator dinged and Zac tugged her on board. "Here? Do you have the equipment to do that? Maybe your friend should go to the hospital to have it checked out."

"It's Dustin—the concierge you saw last night. He refuses to go. Plus, he's diabetic." Zac punched the button for their floor.

"And you tell *me* I work too hard." She snorted. "So how is it that you class Dustin as a friend? You only met him yesterday."

Zac stared down at his shoes. "It's a long story."

"Uh-huh." Carmen crossed her arms and tapped her toe against the carpet. "I've got a long break."

"Let's just say that it's not my first time here at the Arctic Star Resort." The elevator dinged and he gestured for her to exit first. "I've been here before."

"Really?" She looked around at all the opulence. He might be the best EMT in Anchorage, but he still lived on a paramedic's salary. "When?"

"Twelve years ago."

He unlocked the door to their suite and nudged her inside before she could ask any more questions. The fact that the time period was the same as that of his estrangement from his family wasn't lost on her, though. She filed that information away for future reference.

"Carmen Sanchez, this is Dustin Lewis. Carmen and I work together in Anchorage. She's a midwife."

"Ah, nice to meet you Ms. Sanchez," Dustin said, giving her a little bow and a smile. "You must be here for the conference, then."

"I am." She set her tote bag aside. "And please, call me Carmen."

"Okay." Zac grabbed his EMT pack from the bedroom, then returned to set things out on a table: a disposable scalpel, gauze, gloves, sterile field, cotton balls and antiseptic, even a syringe and lidocaine. "Dustin, have a seat here at the table, please. Carmen's going to help me get that cut on your arm cleaned and dressed."

Dustin tried to wave him off. "Don't worry about it, boy. Told you I'm fine."

"That cut is not fine. When you came up to see me this morning and I looked at it I could clearly see it's well on its way to being infected. If you don't nip it in the bud now it could spread to your bloodstream or turn into gangrene, neither of which are pleasant. Trust me, you *want* me to take care of it for you now. After we get it cleaned and dressed, maybe Carmen can write you a script for some antibiotics as well, just to be on the safe side. Do you have any allergies?"

"No. No allergies."

Grumbling, Dustin took a seat and rolled up the sleeve of his dress shirt. Carmen saw the bandage around his lower forearm and had to agree with Zac. Dried blood caked the bandage and the skin around the gauze was red and inflamed.

"Yes, I can write a script. I always bring supplies with me, just in case. Something Zac and I have in common. Let me wash my hands, then I'll get the patient ready for you."

She scrubbed down in the kitchenette sink with the antibacterial soap packet Zac gave her, then put on a pair of gloves and laid out an absorbent pad beneath Dustin's injured arm. She cut away the soiled bandages. Yep. That cut was infected, all right. She poured antiseptic on a cotton ball and prepared to clean the wound as best she could for Zac, prior to the incision.

"Sorry, but this might hurt a bit."

"Nah. Don't feel much anymore, with the nerve damage from my diabetes," Dustin said, giving a dismissive wave with his other hand.

"I suspect that's why we're in this situation now," Zac said to Carmen, his tone low, for her ears only.

"Probably." She cleaned the cut and tossed the cotton balls away in the small red plastic portable biohazard bin from Zac's pack. "All right, Dustin—Zac, ready when you are."

"I know you said you don't feel much," Zac said, drawing lidocaine from the small vial into the syringe, then flicking it a few times with his finger to get any air bubbles out. "But this will numb the area just in case, okay?"

"Whatever, boy," Dustin said, looking the

other way. "Just hurry up and get it over with. You know I don't like needles."

Zac injected the lidocaine around the cut, then scrubbed down himself before putting on fresh gloves and opening the sterile scalpel packet. "Okay. I'm going to drain the wound now. You should feel better after this, Dustin."

The procedure only took a few minutes, and soon Carmen was applying new gauze pads and bandages to Dustin's forearm while Zac finished cleaning up the area. Once the wound was bandaged, Carmen scrubbed her hands and disposed of her gloves, then went into the bedroom to dig her prescription pad out of her bag. She returned to find Zac and Dustin talking in the living room.

"Keep the wound clean and dry and I'll check it again for you tomorrow, to make sure we got all the infection out," Zac said. "You should go see your doctor in town as soon as possible. Or if not him then the traveling physician who comes to the resort, the next time he's here."

"Looks aren't the only thing you got from your daddy, boy. Got his bossiness too," Dustin said, rolling his shirtsleeve back down over the bandage. "But thank you for your help. And you too, Carmen." The older man grinned. "Never did see such a pretty nurse."

"Midwife," Carmen corrected him, then

laughed as she handed him a script for antibiotics. "Make sure you take these with food. You knew Zac's family well, then?"

Zac gave them both a pointed look that all but screamed *Shut up*.

Dustin winked at her. "I did. I *do*. But I should go. I hope you both enjoy your stay at the Arctic Star Resort."

"We will," Carmen said, following him to the door while Zac disappeared into the bedroom.

Her curiosity about his family was growing, given that Dustin knew them, but she'd hesitated to ask with Zac right there. Having him leave for a moment gave her an opportunity she couldn't pass up.

She leaned her shoulder against the doorframe and lowered her voice. "Listen, I'm not trying to pry, but Zac and I are friends and I've noticed that talking about his family really bothers him. In fact, I think being here, period, bothers him. Can you tell me why that is?"

Dustin watched her closely for a second, then glanced over at the bedroom door before answering in a whisper. "I really don't think it's my place to say anything about Zac's personal life. Those are questions you should ask *him*. I will confirm, though, that this place holds a lot of memories for him. Some good, some not so great. But, again, it's not my place to discuss them with you. Sorry."

Carmen sighed, shoulders slumped. Neither she nor Zac had slept well last night. He'd insisted she take the bedroom, and he'd taken the oversized sofa in the living room. They'd both been tired, after the busy day and their walk to the animal reserve, but judging by the number of times she'd heard him up he'd not fared any better than she had sleep-wise.

She'd asked Zac to come this weekend, and now he looked more stressed than she'd ever seen him. Feeling responsible for that, because of dredging up his past, she wanted to do something nice for him. There was no formal dinner tonight, so they had the evening free.

"I'd like to do something nice for Zac tonight. I've not been to this area before, so I'm not sure what's around besides the resort." She tilted her head slightly to catch Dustin's gaze. "You know him better than I do. What would he like?"

Dustin regarded her for a moment, then said, "Bowling."

"Bowling?" She raised a brow. That wasn't what she'd expected.

"He likes to bowl. Used to be pretty good at it too." Dustin crossed his arms, careful to avoid messing up his bandage. "There's an alley in the village not far from here. It's the weekend, so there's probably leagues in there tonight, but if you call ahead they'll take a reservation. I can handle that for you, if you like."

"Oh, yes, please."

Back home in Trinidad, Carmen had used to take Clara bowling at the alley down from their apartment on the nights when their mother had had to work late. It had been light and busy and it had made them feel safer than staying home alone in the evenings. Plus, there'd been a little greasy spoon diner inside, and the owner would slip them free food from time to time. Returning to a bowling alley now, with Zac, would be a nice change of pace. And if it was something he enjoyed, all the better.

"Thanks, Dustin."

"My pleasure. Enjoy your day. And thanks again for helping with my wound."

He left the room and Carmen checked her watch again. "Shoot. I need to get back downstairs for my next seminar," Carmen called out to Zac as she rushed to grab her tote bag from the floor, where she'd set it earlier. "Don't make any plans tonight. I've got something in mind for us."

"Yeah?" Zac looked at her as he came out of the bedroom. "What's that?"

"A secret. One of my own this time." She grinned and headed for the door.

"Great—just what we need. More secrets."

His deep, rich laugh followed her out the door and down the hall to the elevators.

The rest of the day passed in a blur of medical information, an informal lunch interview with Ellen and more seminars with Priya. Carmen's brain ached by the time she returned to the suite at around five, to find Zac working on his computer, but she was looking forward to the night ahead.

"Hey," she said, coming through the door and dumping her heavy tote on a chair in the corner. "What's going on?"

"Not much. Catching up on some emails from work. Inventory time again. Susan's handling it alone," he said, shutting his laptop. "Always stressful."

"Yeah, I'm sure."

She toed off her comfy tennis shoes, then wiggled her toes. Clothing-wise, she was trying to dress professionally for the weekend. Skirt, blazer, white button-down shirt, name badge... But with the running around the large resort all day, from room to room, the comfy shoes were a must.

"I'm going to take a shower, then we can head

out for the night. Make sure you wear something comfortable."

He narrowed his gaze on her again. "No formal dinner tonight? No interview?"

"Nope. I had another brief interview with Ellen earlier. We're on our own tonight."

She took off her blazer and tossed it on the bed in the other room, then returned to the living room. Zac's bedding from the night before was neatly stacked on the corner of the sofa. It felt a bit decadent to have that whole king-sized bed to herself, but the alternative was to share—and, well, that wasn't a good idea either, so…

She cleared her throat and forced her mind away from images of her and Zac entwined in the sheets. He was still watching her with that skeptical look of his and she finally cracked. "Fine. No more secrets from me. You took me to the animal sanctuary last night. This evening I thought we could grab some dinner then maybe go bowling."

"Wait." Zac stood and walked over to her, laughing. "You want to go *bowling*?"

"Sure—why not?"

"No reason. Just never pictured you liking that sort of thing."

"Sometimes people surprise you." She walked to the bathroom door and winked at him. "See you in a sec."

* * *

An hour later Zac held the door for Carmen at the Strike City Alley in town. He hadn't been there since high school, but it still looked the same as he remembered. To the right was an arcade. To the left was the snack bar. In the center was the counter where you paid and got your shoe rentals. Closer to the alleys were racks of balls of all colors and weights.

He still had a hard time imagining Carmen being comfortable in a place like this. But then he remembered her talking to Dustin earlier and wondered if his old friend had something to do with it. Otherwise there was no way Carmen would know about Strike City.

The bowling alley was in a nondescript building on a side street in the middle of nowhere. In fact, he'd loved coming here as a kid because people hadn't treated him differently in this place. They hadn't cared that he was rich and black. The owners had been Inuit and they hadn't cared less what their patrons looked like or what they believed or who they slept with, only that they were respectful and paid their bill.

Carmen gave her name at the counter and was given their lane assignment along with red, white and blue rental shoes for each of them. After changing, Zac stood to watch the other bowlers in the packed alley. Most were in leagues and were very good. The scoreboards overhead listed all the teams and their rankings.

"You want to eat first?" He looked down at Carmen, who was still tying her shoes.

"Whatever you want. We've got the lane until closing, so there's time."

"Great."

Zac escorted her to the snack bar and went to the counter to order them a large plate of nachos to split and two sodas. Once the food was ready he carried the tray to the tall round table where Carmen sat. Music pulsed through the overhead speakers, adding to the fun, slightly chaotic atmosphere.

Carmen dug into the food, humming as she did so.

Zac chuckled as she bopped along in her chair while she ate, licking a drop of cheese from the corner of her mouth and giving him all sorts of naughty ideas.

Carmen looked up and caught him watching her. "What?"

"Nothing."

His gaze dropped to her mouth again before he looked away. He should *not* be remembering their kiss from last night. Especially since he'd spent most of the afternoon trying to avoid those memories and failing miserably.

He'd gone for a swim, then a run, then a massage, then gone back to the suite to fiddle with his computer and check his emails. Nothing had helped. She was in his system again, like a drug, and the chemistry between them was addictive. Maybe more so because he knew damned well he was playing with fire where she was concerned.

Carmen was a risk to his heart he shouldn't take.

And if his raging libido would get with the program he'd be all set.

She continued eating, licking more cheese off her lips, and damn if he didn't have to bite back a groan. He'd been glad to go out tonight, thinking being away from the resort and out in the open would help him relieve some of his stress and help him keep his hands to himself where Carmen was concerned. But it seemed this evening was only going to make things more difficult.

He did his best to concentrate on his own plate after that. "Have you bowled before?" he asked.

"Yep. Used to take my sister to the bowling alley by our apartment when we were growing up. I was pretty good back then. Won a lot of money off the tourists who didn't think a girl could make strikes like I did."

"Really?" He ate faster, to distract himself from the image of Carmen fleecing a bunch of unsuspecting tourists through her skill, wits and determination. Somehow, knowing she had a naughty side just made her sexier, if that were possible. "Well, I was pretty good too, in my day. Looks like we'll have a battle on our hands."

"Bring it on." She sipped her soda and gave him a sly smile, her green-gold eyes sparkling with attitude. "Ready when you are."

He shook his head and ate three chips at once. "Not yet. Finish your food first."

"Agreed." She devoured another chip, then looked around the bowling alley. "This place is a lot nicer than the one I used to go to back home. The walls there clashed with the floor and it reeked of cigarette smoke and booze."

"Doesn't sound like a good place for kids to hang out." Despite his dad's issues, Zac had grown up privileged. From what he knew about Carmen now, she hadn't. In fact, he couldn't imagine growing up in the kind of poverty Carmen had experienced. "Wouldn't you have been safer at home?"

"Nah. Our mother did the best she could, but the building we lived in had some pretty shady characters, so being out and around people was a better bet." She shrugged. "What about you? What was it like where you grew up?"

Zac forced his tense shoulders to relax. This wasn't some random person asking him about his past—this was Carmen, his friend. He wouldn't tell her everything, but he found that for the first time in a long time, he wanted to share something.

"It was great. Nice. Not much different than where we are now. My mother was kind and caring. My dad worked a lot when I was younger, so I didn't see him that much. We had a good life."

She hesitated, then asked, "But then your father had an affair?"

His instinct was to shut down, but he forced himself to continue. "Yeah. When I was sixteen. Everything changed after that."

"Oh, Zac. I'm so sorry." Carmen set her soda aside and reached over to take his hand.

He nodded. "He betrayed my trust, betrayed my mother. I couldn't forgive him for that. Still can't. He was my idol. I wanted to be like him when I grew up. Always thought I would be. Then he told us he'd made a mistake and slept with another woman. That's not a mistake. A mistake is when you forget to pick up the dry cleaning or buy the wrong kind of toothpaste. Not when you end up in bed with someone who's not your spouse. An affair is a deliberate act, a conscious choice. How do you forgive something like that?"

"I don't know," she said.

The warmth of her skin against his helped ground him.

"I don't know much about my father," she went on. "He walked out on our family when I was eight. My sister, Clara, was only two, so she barely remembers him, but I do. He was rich. South American. Turned out he had this whole other life back in Argentina we knew nothing about. Once he walked out the door my mother never heard from him again. No money, no child support. Nothing. It's like we didn't exist. Like he'd erased us from his life."

Zac entwined his fingers with hers, his throat tight. No wonder she felt the way she did about wealthy people. "I'm sorry too."

"It's fine." She sighed and sat back, pulling her hand away. "We were better off without him. If that's how he treated people, he didn't deserve us."

"Amen. You're too good for him." Zac toasted her with his soda cup.

"My mother is a saint. I owe her everything for taking care of us like she did, for the sacrifices she made on our behalf." Carmen tapped her cup against his, then exhaled slowly. "So, what about your mother? I know you don't speak with your father, but she must miss you very much. You left her behind when you left?"

He flinched slightly. "I had to. She made her choice and I made mine. Out of respect to her, I couldn't stay there. So I moved to Anchorage. Put myself through school. Like I said before, I originally planned to be a doctor, but then I volunteered with the local ambulance authority to get more experience under my belt and fell in love with it. I decided to focus on a paramedic career instead. It was the right decision for me. I've never looked back."

"Hmm… Interesting."

"What?" He frowned.

"Most people would consider forgiveness a *good* thing. Your mother was able to move past something like that and continue loving your father, strengthening her marriage to him. The mark of a solid bond, in my opinion." She shrugged. "Not that you asked for my opinion."

Her sweet smile took away a bit of the sting of her words, though tension still coiled inside him like a spitting cobra. Zac wasn't used to having his decisions analyzed and second-guessed. In his work, making clear, concise, correct decisions meant the difference between life and death. In his private life… Well, he'd never really talked to anyone about his family situation before, so all this felt more than a bit uncomfortable, to say the least.

Plus, the mental picture he had of his poor mom sitting there, pining away for him, didn't sit well with him either. She would've moved on by now, right? His father ran a multi-billion-dollar empire. There wouldn't be time for her to miss him.

Except the pinch in his heart told him maybe that wasn't the case.

Before he could dwell too long over the past, however, Carmen broke into his thoughts, forcing him to focus on the conversation at hand.

"I feel the same way about midwifery that you do about being an EMT. I can't imagine having another career. I love being there when new life enters the world. Plus, being a midwife allows me to get involved in my patients' lives. Not to disparage the OB-GYNs, but they usually have such large patient loads, and all the extra paperwork and regulations. No, thank you. I'm happy in my niche." She smiled and snagged the last nacho from the plate. "That's why this California job seems so perfect. Aside from the money, it would give me a chance to do more of what I love and pay it forward—to help the next generation find their place in this career I love."

"Good for you. And I've signed on to teach

some certification classes for EMTs at the local vocational college this spring." He leaned back in his chair, satisfied. Not just from the food, but from the company too. "I want to give back to the job that's given me so much."

They were from opposite ends of the spectrum. They shouldn't have worked. And yet he felt more connected to Carmen right now than he ever had to anyone else.

Which meant it was definitely time to start bowling.

Zac stood and disposed of their trash, then led Carmen down to their lane. There were two more days left of this conference and he didn't want to mess things up between them by taking her to bed again. Best to ignore the growing flames between them and the strengthening connection and keep to their original plan.

Carmen had selected a ball from the racks and set it in the return. Zac did the same. While she typed their names into the scoring system he picked up his own ball and eyed the pins. "Should we take a couple of practice rounds?"

"Go ahead." She gave him a cocky grin. "If you think it will help."

Considering he was practically vibrating with desire for her, it couldn't hurt. Maybe he could burn off enough of his excess energy to bowl a decent game that way.

After a deep breath to calm himself down, he sent the ball down the lane, managing to knock over all but one pin on his first try. Perhaps he hadn't lost his magic after all.

He took out that last pin on his next shot, then sat behind the screen while Carmen took her practice turn. Sure enough, she bowled a perfect strike. Pride and passion zinged through him. He did love a woman who could handle herself well.

She walked back, her expression brimming with challenge. "Let's do this."

He didn't miss the double-entendre in her words or the spark of heat in her eyes. Despite knowing better, he gave in to the attraction simmering inside him, allowing it to roll into a full boil. "Whatever you want, darling."

"Darling, huh?" she said, winking. "Just for that, I'm going to beat you even worse."

And by the end of the night she'd done just that.

Zac had honestly bowled his best game ever, but she'd still trounced him—and he'd enjoyed every minute of it. In truth, he couldn't remember having a better night.

They changed back into their street shoes, then took a cab back to the resort. Carmen was quiet during the ride, sitting closer to him in the back seat of the compact than was necessary, but Zac wasn't complaining. Her heat and the press of her soft curves against him only served to notch his pulse higher. His skin felt too tight for his body and his nerve-endings prickled with awareness.

At the hotel, they walked quickly through the lobby and over to the elevators. The doors swished shut, leaving them alone.

Carmen turned to Zac at last, and the need in her eyes matched his own. "Look, I know we agreed not to sleep together again this weekend, but—"

He kissed her before she finished her sentence. She tasted sweet from her soda and spicy from the jalapeños on the nachos. Her hands skimmed up his chest to twine around his neck and he gripped her hips, his fingers digging into the denim of her jeans as she arched against him. Her tongue tangled with his and she ground against him, one leg looping around his waist as if she couldn't get close enough.

He was tempted to hit the stop button and have her right there, up against the mirrored wall of the elevator, but Carmen deserved better. She deserved the suite and the king-sized bed and the expensive sheets. She deserved every good and wonderful thing, and he intended to see she got it—at least for tonight.

Ding!

"C'mon," Zac growled, tugging her toward their room. "I want you, Carmen. So badly I ache."

She nodded, keeping up with him step for step. "And I want you too."

CHAPTER EIGHT

CARMEN SHED HER parka the minute she and Zac
tumbled through the door in a mass of limbs
and kisses. The rest of her clothes followed suit,
until she was left in just her bra and panties. Her
whole body burned for him.

And, yes, maybe sleeping with him again was
a bad decision, but she'd denied the connection
and chemistry between them for days—months.
There was no more denying it now. Tomorrow
she'd go back to devoting all her time to others.
Tonight was just for her.

He took off his jacket as well and tossed it
aside, then tugged his sweater over his head,
leaving his muscled torso bare. He stalked toward her slowly, as she inched back toward the
bed, and his hot, greedy gaze roamed over her.

"I didn't think it was possible to want you
any more than I already did, but I was wrong."

"Same."

She gave him a slow smile. The more time

she'd spent with Zac this weekend, and the more she'd learned about him, the more she'd discovered they were more alike than different. He was sexy as hell, yes. But he was also strong, smart, honest and true. Maybe he wasn't Mr. Forever, but he was hers for this weekend.

After crawling onto the bed, Carmen leaned back on her elbows and propped one leg up, letting the other dangle over the edge of the mattress as she crooked her finger at him. "Come here…"

"Yes, ma'am."

The half-growled, half-groaned words only stoked the passion in her blood higher. Zac removed his jeans, then dropped to his knees on the floor beside the bed, taking her hips in his hands and pulling her to the end of the mattress. He leaned in, his broad shoulders forcing her thighs to part wider.

His eyes met hers over the length of her body, and the heat in his stare was brazen. Then he grinned. "This is for beating me at bowling."

The first gentle lick of his tongue across the silk of her panties made Carmen's breath catch. During their one-night stand he'd been an attentive lover. But that had been rushed and they'd both been drunk. Now he seemed more than happy to take all the time in the world. She swallowed hard and closed her eyes, clenching the covers in her hands to keep from crying out in sweet frustration.

Zac slid her panties down her legs, then licked her again, using his fingers to stroke her as well. Carmen arched beneath him, unable to hold back her soft moans of need any longer. He slid one finger inside her, then two, as his tongue nuzzled her most sensitive flesh.

"You're so ready for me," he whispered, the words reverberating through her body.

She slipped a hand down to hold him closer to her. "Zac, please…"

"Please what, darling?" he asked. "Tell me what you want."

"You. I want you."

With a soft growl he kissed his way up her body, his fingers never leaving her slick folds, until he held himself over her. "Say it again. Tell me."

"Please, Zac. I want you."

He reached over and pulled a condom from the nightstand drawer, put it on, then removed her bra, leaving them both naked. "I want you too, Carmen. Are you sure?"

She nodded, and he lifted her hips, pulling her toward him as he thrust forward, filling her completely. Zac stilled, allowing her body to adjust to his. Moments later Carmen rocked forward, letting him know she needed more.

His expression intense, he set up a steady rhythm, his gaze locked with hers. "You feel so incredible. I thought I'd imagined it that first time. Thought it was impossible. But I was wrong. So wrong. You're amazing."

"So are you."

Carmen met him thrust for thrust, giving herself over completely to this man, this moment, this time together. Sweat sheened his forehead as they both teetered on the brink of climax all too soon. His rough groans of mounting pleasure filled the air and her blood pounded in her veins. No matter what issues they had outside of this room, in bed they fit like two pieces of the same puzzle. She wanted this night to go on forever. She wanted him to bring her to orgasm before she couldn't take it anymore.

Pressure built inside her, causing her to grind against him even harder, seeking her own fulfillment. Finally her passion crested, and her world exploded into ecstasy. Zac followed close behind her, his back arching as he thrust into her hard one last time and orgasmed.

Afterward, he collapsed on the bed, his eyes closed and his expression relaxed for the first time she'd seen all weekend. Carmen felt so limp she could barely move. Zac's leg tangled with hers as she turned on her side and laid her hand on his chest.

The sweat on their skin chilled, and he pulled the covers over them, holding her close as she gave him a sleepy grin. "Guess that'll teach me to get more strikes than you, huh?"

He chuckled, tucking her head under his chin. "Nah. I love having a worthy opponent."

Zac wasn't an idiot. He had known as soon as Carmen snuggled atop him and gave a huge contented sigh that he'd made a mistake taking her to bed again. Not because of their stupid fake engagement, but because this was a woman he respected. A woman who was a friend and a colleague. A woman who challenged him on every level.

A woman he could love.

Dammit.

He didn't do love. Love meant trust. Love meant risk. After the disaster he'd witnessed in his parents' relationship he never wanted to leave himself open to that kind of heartache and disappointment. This weekend should've been fun. Lighthearted. Low risk. Then he'd gone and opened up to her more than he should have and they'd connected on a deeper level. Now, he'd let her into his life and his heart in a way he'd never let anyone in a long, long time.

She wanted different things. She'd be moving away soon, if she got the job in California.

She had a life and responsibilities of her own.
Yet he couldn't seem to stop himself from en-
visioning a future with them together. Working
side by side at Anchorage Mercy, getting married, starting a family of their own.

Except there were still so many things she
didn't know about him—his family, his past...

He should have told her the truth before they
slept together again, he knew that, but the time
hadn't seemed right. And then his body had
taken over, and his brain had taken a back seat,
and...*ugh*.

What a mess.

He stroked his fingers through Carmen's
curls, savoring their silky feel against his skin.
Her hair twined around his hand, as if begging
him to stay.

She propped herself up on her elbow to look
at him, a slight frown marring her beautiful
face. "What are you thinking about?"

Zac realized he had another opportunity at
that moment—to let it go or talk about it.

Letting it go would lead to more sex.

Talking about his past would guarantee she
wouldn't want anything more to do with him.

She'd already made it clear she didn't trust
rich people—had no use for them at all after the
way her own wealthy father had behaved and
the way she'd been treated by those entitled frat

boys who'd expected things from her when she'd worked at that luxury resort in Trinidad. Once she found out his father owned this resort, and many more like it, any relationship they might have had would be over.

Torn, Zac rolled onto his side to see her face-to-face. Right or wrong, he wanted them to have the rest of this night together. He'd tell her the truth about himself tomorrow. He *would*. And if it all fell apart then at least he'd have these precious memories to look back on.

"I'm glad we're here together tonight."

"Me too."

She traced her finger down his chest, making him shiver.

"I feel like I can just be myself with you. I don't have to impress you. You're real—normal. Not like some of the men I've come across before. Most guys I've been out with either expected me to take care of them or tried to impress me with their money. But I don't care about that. Wealth doesn't make a man. I learned that lesson all too well with my father."

Zac hid his wince. Yeah, he'd learned that with his father too.

"Although…" Carmen snorted and gestured to the suite around them. "All of this *doesn't* suck."

"True," he said. "But this isn't reality."

"Tonight it is." She gave him a sweet, sexy smile.

He wanted to forget—forget the lies and the past and just enjoy what time they had together here in their little private paradise of a bedroom—but he couldn't.

"Hey, why so serious?" she asked. "We're supposed to be basking in the afterglow."

She nudged him with her shoulder and Zac forced a small smile.

"Listen." She held his hand and toyed with his fingers. "I have no fantasies about money. I've seen the best and worst it can do and I'm careful. My mother and sister and I live frugally, and I don't depend on others to give me what I need. If that's a problem for you, then I'm sorry."

"No, it's not a problem, I just…" He exhaled slowly and held her closer. "Honestly, it makes me respect you even more."

"Good." She smiled. "A lot of men are threatened by an independent woman. I'm glad you're not one of them."

Zac couldn't seem to look away from her. Carmen was gorgeous, no doubt. But now he also saw her inner strength and determination, her confidence and intelligence, and that made her even more beautiful. She worked hard and she deserved the best in life.

His heart squeezed tighter in his chest, and that was when he knew he was a goner—which only scared him more. Still, he pushed past the fear, because she deserved this moment even if he couldn't give her forever. No matter how he might wish otherwise.

"Thank you."

She took a deep breath. "For what?"

"For tonight. For being my friend. For everything."

It didn't cover even half of what he needed to say, the things he needed to tell her, but it was all he could do at the moment.

"You're welcome." She gave him a surprised smile, then raised a brow, the glint in her lovely eyes positively wicked. "You ready for round two?"

Zac felt the blood in his body divert southward. Yep, his heart was definitely a goner where this woman was concerned, and he was well and truly terrified.

He was also not moving out of this bed for anything in the world—not until he had no other choice. He leaned in and kissed her deeply. "More than ready."

CHAPTER NINE

ZAC WAS UP before Carmen the next morning. Which was good, because if she'd rolled over and smiled at him he'd never have wanted to leave her side. And he needed to go. Needed to get some space and clear his mind.

The fact was, last night was messing with his head. This was supposed to be a fun weekend. No commitments. No strings attached. And while it had certainly been fun, feelings were stirring inside him. Feelings that shouldn't be there—tenderness, longing, satisfaction, sweetness. Feelings beyond like and nearing...

No. He wasn't going there.

They were friends. Good friends. Friends with benefits.

But the more he got to know Carmen, the more he wanted from her.

He went into the bathroom and pulled on his swim trunks, careful to be quiet and avoid waking her. Then he went back out into the bedroom to grab a clean pair of jeans and a T-shirt from his bag, to put on after his time in the pool. There were changing rooms downstairs and he didn't plan to come back to the suite until after she'd left for the day.

It was avoidance, plain and simple, but then "mornings-after" weren't exactly his thing.

Usually he was long gone by the time the sun rose on his flings. It was only being honest, really. He wasn't cut out for relationships—not with the example his father had set for him—and he always told his partners that up front.

He'd told Carmen that too, but something about this weekend with her had changed things. Made him think that maybe he'd been lying to himself all along. Made him wonder if perhaps settling down was what he wanted and needed, but he wasn't brave enough to try for it. Because if a man like his father had been seduced into cheating, who was to say Zac wouldn't make the same mistake? And the last thing he wanted to do was hurt Carmen. She'd been through enough in her life already.

Torn and twisted inside, he let himself out of the room and headed downstairs. Sleeping with Carmen again didn't feel like just another one-night stand. Being with her felt like champagne and breakfast in bed. Like lazy Sunday mornings reading the paper.

Like a "forever" kind of thing.

Too bad he was just a "right now" kind of guy.

Aren't I?

This early in the morning there weren't many people up and about at the resort, so he had the pool to himself. For half an hour he did laps, working out some of the tension that had been building in his muscles for days and hoping the time alone might do the same for his jumbled mind.

By the time he'd finished and pulled himself out to sit on the edge of the pool, he was out of breath and shaking from exertion—and still remembering Carmen upstairs in bed, tousled and tempting as hell. Instead of racing back there, like he wanted, he jumped back in the water to put in another twenty minutes.

But even the burn of his body as he pushed it to its limits didn't stop the sound of her gasps as he'd brought her to climax again and again, the taste of salt from her skin, the feel of her exquisite breasts in his palms.

There was no doubt the two of them fit perfectly—in and out of bed.

She'd been a delight at the bowling alley—laughing and teasing and pushing him to do better, to be better, because she was so good. He still couldn't quite believe he'd opened up to her as much as he had about his past and his father—more than he had with anyone else in recent memory. And even with all she'd told him about herself he wanted to know more. He wanted to know what she ate for breakfast, what toothpaste she liked, how she got her hair to stay in those perfect curls, who had been her first crush and could he possibly be her last...if he was brave enough to try?

Damn.

He dunked himself underwater, then rose to swipe his hand over his face. Enough. Brave or not, all this was pointless. Because after this weekend he'd go back to his life in Anchorage and she'd most likely be moving to California. Nothing would change, because nothing *could* change.

Zac climbed out of the pool and grabbed his towel from a nearby chair. He dried off, then headed into the changing rooms to shower and pull on the clothes he'd brought.

Wishing things were different would get him exactly nowhere. He didn't like to think about his father or his upbringing often, but in this instance his father's words rang true.

Get over it, son.

Intent on doing just that, after he was dressed Zac decided to hit the resort restaurant for breakfast. Usually, when he was at home and working, he ate on the run. He never knew when a call would come in and he had to be ready in a moment's notice. Today, though, he planned to order the most elaborate thing on the menu— just to burn up some time. Whatever took the longest to cook, that was what he'd have. Then, once he'd eaten, he'd stop by the front desk, just to confirm that Carmen had gone to her seminars for the day before returning to the suite.

It wasn't that he was afraid he wouldn't be able to keep his hands to himself—though the idea of keeping her in bed all day was more than appealing. Nope. What kept him out of the room and away from her was the very real and terrifying possibility that she'd want to talk more, find out more about him. Because that was the thing about secrets. Once you opened the door even a little the whole mess had a tendency to spill out.

He berated himself again for not being honest with her up front, even though it would do him little good now. What was done was done, and the only way to move was forward.

Get over it, son.

He rounded the corner and halted at the entrance to the restaurant. It was Saturday, and he'd forgotten they only served a buffet breakfast on the weekend. *Damn.* That cut out any prep time for his food. Fine. He'd eat slowly. It was all good.

The hostess showed him to a table for two in the mainly empty dining room, then directed him to help himself at the buffet.

He was doing just that when a familiar voice said from beside him, "Morning, boy."

Dustin.

Zac glanced at the older gentleman and smiled, grateful for the distraction. "Good morning. How's the arm?"

"Better. Thanks to you and your lady friend."

Dustin let him see the bandage, then toasted him with his cup of coffee. Zac's father had always given the employees complimentary meals during their shifts. *A perk of the job,* his dad had always said. *Treat people right and they'll do the same for you.*

Too bad his good judgment hadn't carried over to his marriage or his family.

"Where is the lovely Carmen this morning?" Dustin asked, picking up several slices of bacon with a pair of tongs while Zac loaded his plate with hash browns and eggs.

He rolled his shoulders to ease the knots between his shoulder blades and forced a smile he didn't quite feel. "Carmen's not my lady friend. She's just a friend. And she's still in the room, as far as I know."

"I see… But she is lovely, though." Dustin cocked his head, as though he saw right through the BS, then headed toward a table not far from Zac's. "Why don't you join me?"

"Sure—if you don't mind?"

"If I minded I wouldn't have asked." Dustin chuckled and walked away.

Zac followed the older man to his table, where there was already a pot of coffee and a carafe of orange juice waiting. They sat down and started on their food.

"Seen your parents yet?" Dustin asked.

"Nah." Zac halted mid-bite and shook his head. "Had a near miss Thursday night, but I managed to get out of the banquet room before they saw me."

"You know you can't outrun them forever, boy?"

Yeah, Zac knew. But if he could just avoid a confrontation this weekend, that would be great. He didn't want to ruin things for Carmen. Didn't want to deal with all the pain and hurt and regret himself, either.

He stared down at his plate, his appetite plummeting. He felt like the walls were closing in on him and he didn't like it one bit.

"Maybe you should just talk to him," Dustin said, watching Zac over the rim of his coffee cup. "Get it over with."

"No." He pushed around a mound of potatoes with his fork. "I've got nothing to say to him."

"Really?" The older man remained silent for a moment, then said, "My employment anniversary here is coming up next month. Been at the Arctic Star for twenty-nine years. Almost as long as your father has owned the place."

"Congratulations." Zac didn't look up, even though he could feel Dustin's gaze on him. This wasn't a conversation he wanted to have right now.

"I still remember that night you tore out of here after talking to your dad that last time. He was devastated after you left—kept trying to get ahold of you, but you wouldn't take his calls. I think he aged a hundred years in a month back then. Hard times."

Well, at least that last part was right. "Hard" didn't begin to describe the anger and betrayal Zac had felt after learning of his dad's affair. He'd spent sixteen years idolizing the man, following in his footsteps, wanting to be just like him. To have all that demolished over one stupid, thoughtless decision had been something he just couldn't forgive and forget.

Of course the media circus that had followed the story breaking hadn't helped either. The stupid tabloids had brought it up over and over again, rubbing their family's faces in it. In fact, it had been after reading a particularly heinous smear piece about his father that Zac had wrecked his car and put his date in the hospital. He'd thought he could outrun the rage and embarrassment, but that hadn't been the case.

It was never the case. Problems had a way of following you until you dealt with them, once and for all.

"He's missed you terribly," Dustin said. "We all have."

"Yeah, well… He should've thought about that before he did what he did." Zac shook his head. "Please don't preach at me about forgiveness. What he did was wrong and now he has to live with the consequences. I know my mother was able to move past it, and I respect her decision, but I'm not there yet."

"Not disagreeing with you there, boy. Infidelity is an ugly thing. But we all stumble sometimes. It's what we do afterward that counts."

Dustin finished his coffee, then checked his watch and stood.

"Time for me to finish up back at the desk and turn things over to Willow for the day shift. I'll be around later if you need me. Think about making amends, boy. Time is precious. Don't waste new opportunities because of old tribulations."

With that, the older man walked away, leaving Zac alone to stare after him.

Frowning, he finished his food and thought over Dustin's words. As far as Zac knew, his sixty-year-old father was in fine health. Honestly, the man was stubborn enough to live to a thousand just to spite the world. Besides, Zac wasn't in much of a forgiving mood at the moment.

He had too many other things on his mind.

Like how to tell the woman he was falling for that he'd been lying to her from the start.

Carmen's day had been filled with more seminars and another lunch meeting with Ellen Landon—this time to discuss the staffing requirements of the new clinic and the newly minted outreach program for providing medical care and prenatal services to the low-income and homeless population in and around Big Sur.

When asked for her opinions, Carmen had spoken from the heart about growing up poor, and how that had given her a special insight into the problems of women living below the poverty line. It was an insight she knew Priya would not be able to share, since she'd grown up in a wealthy family near Chicago. Ellen had been impressed, and for the first time Carmen had felt like she had the upper hand on the new position in California.

That alone should've made her overjoyed. It was what this weekend was all about, after all. What she'd been working so hard toward for the last two months.

But, unfortunately, all she could think about was Zac.

Waking up alone hadn't been how she'd wanted to start the day. Since then she'd kept an eye out for Zac in the halls between seminars, but so far there'd been no sign of him at all. If they'd been back in Anchorage she'd have suspected he was avoiding her. Here at the resort, however, there were plenty of fun activities to take up his time. She'd see him eventually, since the big final banquet was tonight.

The banquet where Ellen would announce her choice for the new job.

An odd mix of nervous butterflies and sad disappointment fluttered through her system. The nerves were about the job. She still wanted it. Of course she did. It was everything she'd dreamed of achieving—more prestige and more responsibility, more opportunities to help those in need, more money to help with her sister's education and her mother's medical care. It was all good.

Except…

She'd miss Anchorage, the people and the places she'd come to love, including Zac. He was her friend, her colleague, her lover.

Yes, he'd made it clear he wasn't the type of man to settle down, but the truth was she'd not been with anyone else since their one night together after the holiday party. It wasn't that she hadn't had cravings, it was just that they'd all been focused on one man, and she doubted anyone else could measure up to the incredible synergy she had with Zac.

Each time she closed her eyes it was like she was right back there with him, riding that wave of pleasure to its ultimate crest. They hadn't been able to get enough of each other and she'd loved every delicious minute of it. He was a generous lover, vocal in what he wanted and expecting the same from her. Part of her had thought maybe sleeping with him again might get him out of her system once and for all, but the opposite was true. She wanted him now more than ever. Being with Zac was addictive and she never wanted to stop.

It was like they were two halves of the same whole.

Which both thrilled and terrified her.

Mainly because she wasn't sure he'd ever admit the same, even though it was obvious he felt it in the way he touched her, held her, knew what she needed before she even knew herself.

Plus, she wasn't used to relying on another person for anything—including love.

But with Zac things seemed deeper, more permanent than in any of her previous relationships. If you could call what they had a relationship. Okay, maybe not a relationship, but the start of...*something*. Something more and special and real.

He'd finally opened up to her at the bowling alley, and later on in bed, sharing glimpses of his past, which was encouraging. And though she sensed he was still holding back secrets, the rest would come with time.

Carmen wasn't one for hearts and rainbows and flower petal romances. She was far too pragmatic. But Zac had well and truly swept her off her feet and now she needed to figure out how to proceed. They needed to talk. She needed to find out what he wanted, since before this weekend he'd made it clear that he was a player.

She wasn't naïve enough to think a night or two of great sex would change a man. Besides, it wasn't her responsibility to fix him, no matter how his broken parts might call to her. But things had moved well past the friend zone for her after last night, and she had to know if they had for him as well.

The clock on the wall said her next seminar was starting soon, so she finished up her coffee, then headed into a talk on using a physiological model for the management of the head-to-body interval during vaginal birth. It was another packed room, but Priya had saved her a seat.

"Hey." Carmen got out her notebook. "How's your day going?"

"Fine," Priya said, although her normally perky tone was flat. "And yours?"

"Good." Carmen glanced over at her and saw her friend was looking a bit green around the gills. "Everything okay?"

"Fine," Priya said. "Just tired."

Unconvinced, Carmen dug a packet of saltine crackers out of her tote. "Here. These will settle your stomach."

"Thanks."

The lights dimmed and the presentation started, but thoughts of the night before continued to distract Carmen. In terms of her career, she probably shouldn't even be looking for anything long-term right now, since she was closer than ever to landing the California job. To turn her back on all that over a man who might not even want her in his future was ludicrous.

No. They needed to talk. And as soon as she could get some alone time with him, they would. If not today, then tonight—at the banquet.

CHAPTER TEN

THE EVENING FINALLY ARRIVED, but for Zac it felt like anything but a party. After avoiding Carmen and his parents for most of the day, and running the conversation he'd had with Dustin over and over in his head on an endless loop, he felt the burden of the secrets he was keeping weighing heavier than ever on his shoulders.

He should tell Carmen the truth.

He wanted to tell Carmen the truth.

He would tell Carmen the truth when the right time came.

Which wasn't now.

After the big announcement about who was to get the new job in California maybe.

In Zac's mind, Carmen was a shoo-in. She was more than qualified, had the practical experience, and most of all she truly cared about her patients and her coworkers. She deserved it. And he intended to do everything he could tonight to make sure she got it—even if it meant losing her forever.

Zac adjusted his black bow tie in the full-length mirror in the suite, then stared at his reflection. Elegant, refined, the designer tux would provide excellent armor for the evening ahead.

We all stumble sometimes. It's what we do afterward that counts.

Exhaling slowly, Zac walked over to the dresser to grab his cufflinks—small ovals of sterling silver engraved with his initials. They were one of the few things he'd taken with him when he'd left this place—a gift from his mother on his high school graduation. They'd cost more than some people made in a week. A reminder of everything he'd left behind.

He slid them into place, then tweaked his cuffs to be sure they were secure.

Moments later Carmen emerged from the bathroom, and he turned to face her...

"Wow," was all he managed to say, taking in the silver beaded lace evening gown that clung like a second skin to all her glorious curves.

Zac swallowed hard against the tightness in his throat. She wore her hair up again too, with a few loose curls hanging around her neck and face. All he could think about was holding her, kissing her, feeling her beneath him, surrounding him as she came apart in his arms.

Carmen put in her earrings—small, sparkling studs—then walked over and turned her back to him. She gave him a coy smile over her shoulder, the glint in her lovely eyes saying she knew exactly the effect she had on him.

"Can you zip me up please?"

Zac did as she asked, his hands far less steady than he'd like. Finished, he stepped back—away from her and her sweet jasmine scent, away from temptation. Because if he didn't keep his distance now they'd both end up back in bed and miss the dinner entirely.

"Are you ready?" She grabbed her tiny purse from the top of the dresser, then gave him a hesitant smile. "We don't want to be late."

"No." He shook his head. "I mean, yes. I'm ready. But before we go…" He took her hands, his pulse pounding in his ears and his skin prickling with heat.

Tell her.

But he couldn't. Not yet. This was her big night.

He'd wait until after the ball, when they were alone, when he would be able to suffer the humiliation and pain of her walking away in private.

She looked up at him, so beautiful, so trusting. He wanted her more than he'd ever wanted any woman in his life, but he'd never be worthy of her.

He cleared his throat. "You look amazing. You'll get that California job and take the entire state by storm. I'll be in Anchorage, cheering you on."

Something flickered in her eyes, gone before he could catch it. If he didn't know better, he'd say it was longing. But then she put on the brave, professional smile he knew so well from Anchorage Mercy and gave a decisive nod.

"Thank you. Let's get downstairs."

The event planners at the resort had certainly outdone themselves with tonight's décor. Zac took it all in as he escorted Carmen into the dining room. LED lights projected a gorgeous display of deep blue, purple and rose colors onto the vaulted ceiling, making it resemble an abstract stained-glass window. Long swathes of white tulle were draped between the columns in the room, stretching from each column to the large chandelier at the center of the space.

The tables had been arranged in semicircles before the stage, where the podium sat ready for the presentations and the big announcement later in the evening. Towering centerpieces of white lilies and roses graced each white-linen-covered table and a tasteful string quartet played in one corner. There was also DJ equipment for later, when the dance floor would open again.

Seemed his father had thought of every detail—again.

Zac's steps faltered and Carmen gave him a curious glance.

"Okay?" she asked, her expression concerned. "You seem more jittery than me tonight."

"I'm fine."

He resisted the urge to fidget with his tie again and scanned the area. Lots of the guests were milling about, talking or laughing or catching up with colleagues they saw only perhaps once a year. No sign of his parents yet, which was a relief. If he'd been here with anyone other than Carmen he would've left, but he didn't want to let her down.

Jaw set, he led Carmen to their table, near the front of the space, held her chair for her, then took the space beside her. Ellen and Liz were there already, as were Priya and Lance.

Zac greeted them all, noting that Lance wasn't acting like his usual outgoing, gregarious self. He seemed hyper-focused on Priya. Doting, even, with his head bent toward her and his arm around her protectively. Zac wanted to ask him what was going on, but the master of ceremonies for the evening had taken the podium to welcome everyone and announce that dinner was served.

While they ate, several presentations took place, and Zac kept a watchful eye out for his father. The thought of playing cat and mouse with him all night had lessened his appetite significantly, though the food was delicious—as always. Sweet potato, coconut and coriander soup for the appetizer, followed by pan-fried duck breast with black cherries and basil polenta, and finishing with raspberry mousse and homemade chocolate-dipped shortbread.

Lovely as the meal was, though, Zac could've been eating cardboard for all he tasted it.

"This resort has been lovely," Ellen said as the waiter cleared away their plates. "I'd definitely come back here for a vacation. If I can tear my wife away from her practice."

Liz laughed, finishing her last bite of raspberry mousse. "I think you could twist my arm. Besides, we should have more free time after this new position at the clinic is filled." She looked over at Carmen, then Priya, giving them each a wink. "Isn't that right?"

"Yes, ma'am," Carmen said.

Priya nodded and gave a wan smile.

Yeah, there was something definitely off with those two. Zac couldn't put his finger on it, but the shadows beneath Priya's eyes suggested that she hadn't been sleeping well. He'd have to pull his buddy aside later and ask. Maybe it would distract him from his own problems.

"Oh, look." Ellen raised her chin toward the opposite side of the dining room as some of the diners began to get up and mill around the room and the buzz of conversation filled the air. "Here comes the owner. We should tell them how much we've enjoyed the venue this year. Oh, but the MC is waving us up to the stage. If you'll excuse us?"

Both she and Liz left before Zac's parents could come over and he felt the earth disappear beneath his feet. If he could've sunk beneath the table he would have.

Instead, he stood and excused himself. "I need some air."

"You can't leave." Carmen frowned up at him. "They're going to make the announcement soon."

"I won't be long," he said, tossing his napkin on the table and stepping back—just as his father approached their table.

Damn. Too late.

They locked eyes for the first time in twelve years and Zac saw his father's expression shift from recognition to determination in a matter of seconds. Zac opened his mouth to speak, but the words stuck in his throat. Vaguely he was aware of Priya excusing herself and heading to the restrooms with Lance following close behind her. Time seemed to slow.

His father continued to stare at him, but his mother was still speaking to a woman at another table nearby. Pulse racing, Zac fisted his hands at his sides and forced himself to stand his ground. This moment had been a long time coming and the air around their table seemed to crackle with tension.

"Son," his father said, his cool tone edged with wariness.

Fresh anger sizzled beneath Zac's skin even as he battled to keep it under control. This was not how he wanted things to go down. Not here. Not now. Not with so much on the line for him.

Carmen glanced between Zac and his father, frowning. "Son...? Zac, what's he talking about? Do you know this man?"

"I did. Once," he said, his jaw tight. "But he has no right to call me that anymore."

His mother turned at that moment, to see her son and her husband facing off across the table. Her bright smile faltered as she took Zac's father's arm. "Please, Zac. It's been so long since we've seen you. Can't we talk about this? Finally put it behind us?"

His father spoke again. "Yes. That's what I want too, son. I'm sorry about what happened all those years ago. It was never my intention to hurt you," his father said, his voice beseeching. "But things are different now. *I'm* different. Please give me a chance to talk to you, to explain things—"

"Zac?" Carmen said, her eyes widening. "Are these your parents?"

Chest aching, Zac stepped away from her. "Yes."

Hurt flickered across her lovely face as she put the pieces together. "Your father owns this resort? Why didn't you tell me?"

"Because I don't tell anyone about my past." His sharp tone reverberated through the space between them. "Why would that be any different this weekend with you?"

Even as the words emerged he regretted them. He had opened up to her more than he had with anyone else. He had even intended to tell her the full truth about himself eventually. But it was too late to take back his statement now, if the way the color had drained from Carmen's face was any indication.

He wanted to apologize, wanted to scream to the huge pine rafters above that he loved her, that none of this mattered to him anymore. All he cared about was her. But it was too late.

Frustrated, he lashed out at his father again. "What exactly are you going to explain to me, huh? How you're a reformed liar and a cheat? How you've moved past your deception and made a new life for yourself with my mother? How you regret throwing away your family, your flesh and blood, and the love of a woman who worshipped the ground you walked on for one night of pleasure? Sorry, but I've already heard it and I can do without the replay. There was a time I worshipped you, trusted you, loved you. But no more. Because not a day goes by that I don't worry I'll turn out just like you. Does that make you proud? Is that the legacy you wanted to pass on to your son? Loneliness? Isolation? Embarrassment? If so, then congratulations. Because of you I don't trust anyone. Because of you I sleep around and never commit to anyone. Why should I when I could end up cheating on them just like you did my mother?"

The truth cut like a razor on Zac's tongue, but he'd been holding it in far too long.

His father's face had gone ashen. "Please, son…"

"Stop calling me that!" Zac pulled away when Carmen reached for his arm.

"Zac, please… Step outside with us into the hallway, where we can discuss this in private," his mother pleaded. "Your father has atoned for his mistakes. He's not the same person. Give him a chance—"

"No. No more chances. He had a chance twelve years ago. To choose to stay faithful to you and the commitment he made to you and his family. But he chose to throw all that away."

Zac glanced over at Carmen, who was watching their exchange. Dots of color had returned to her cheeks and her eyes glittered with angry heat. His heart stumbled anew. This was her special night, the whole reason he was here, and now it was ruined. Because of him. Because of his lies and his deception. He really was no better than his father.

The worst wasn't over, however, because his father had regained some composure and was not backing down.

"You want to do this here? Now? Fine," his father said, his dark eyes glittering with determination. "I've got nothing to hide. All my secrets were laid bare for the world years ago. But can you say the same, son? I've apologized for what I did. I've made amends. I've tried to live better since. People are fallible, son. We fall down. We make mistakes. What happened back then was a horrible mistake on my part, but I've spent every day since making reparation to your mother. We put it behind us and made a new future—a better future. One I'd hoped you'd be a part of. But I can see now that the real thing you inherited from me was stubbornness. You're alone? You're afraid to commit? You don't trust people? Take a look at your own choices, son, before you go laying that on me. I talked to Dustin this evening. He told me about you and your lady friend, here, staying in the suite upstairs. You think I don't see that engagement ring on her finger? Were you planning on even inviting us to the wedding?"

"There is no wedding," Zac said, before he could think better of it. But thankfully, Lance and Priya were still gone and Ellen and Liz were up on the stage. "We faked an engagement so Carmen could get a job she wants in California. Not that it's any of your business. We're just friends. Nothing more."

He'd meant for that chilly statement to put the quick kibosh on his parents' questions about his relationship with Carmen, but he didn't miss the tiny pained gasp from the woman beside him. Zac hid his own wince and hazarded a sideglance at her.

"We'll talk about it later," he whispered. "In our room. Alone."

"Why?" Carmen asked, her arms crossed and her toe tapping against the plush carpet beneath her high-heeled sandals. "You seem to have no problem airing all your dirty laundry right here in front of everyone. Why not this too?"

"Because I'm trying to stick to our deal

and keep your secret," Zac said, keeping his voice down.

"Secrets and fake engagements, eh?" his father said, narrowing his gaze. "Looks like you've got your own issues to deal with. Can't go blaming all this on *me*, son."

"I said don't call me that," Zac growled.

"Don't talk to your parents that way," Carmen said, scowling.

"Stay out of this. It's a private matter. It doesn't concern you."

Zac's heart pinched at the way Carmen blanched, but *dammit*. This was getting out of control. He needed to keep things separate. He needed to regain his cool composure. He needed to sort through all this and find the right way forward.

Unfortunately there was no time to do any of that, because the next thing he heard was the voice of the MC, booming over the PA system in the dining hall.

"And now a special announcement from the primary sponsor of this year's conference— esteemed businesswoman and midwife, and lifelong advocate for women's health, Ellen Landon!"

The master of ceremonies stepped aside and applause filled the dining room. Carmen did her best to hide the hurricane of emotions swirling inside her—hurt, anger, regret, heartache. She took a deep breath and forced herself to smile, since all eyes were focused on her at that moment.

This whole mess was her fault. Zac was right. He was trying to stick to the deal they'd made at the beginning of this whole fiasco. He was her rent-a-fiancé for the weekend, her fake fiancé. It was her own stupid fault that she'd read more into it than she should. Last night had been special to her, but obviously to him it had been just another quick fling.

"Doh eat de bread de devil knead," as her mama would say.

This was a tough time. One of her own making, unfortunately. She'd gone ahead and opened her heart to Zac—gone ahead and fallen for him when he'd clearly shown he didn't want that.

Stupid, Carmen. So stupid.

Lance and Priya returned to the table at last, holding hands and keeping very much to themselves, as they'd done all evening. Strange, that, but Carmen had bigger problems to deal with at the moment.

Ellen smiled down from the podium. "Tonight, we're pleased to announce the candidate we've chosen to be the new head of midwife staff at our Big Sur, California, clinic. It came down to two final contenders—Ms. Priya Shaw and Ms. Carmen Sanchez. Ladies, please stand so we can give you both a round of applause."

Carmen was only vaguely aware of the cheers around her as Zac stood stiffly by her side, not looking at her at all. She wanted to shake him, and she wanted to hug him. She wanted to demand that he tell her why he'd not told her about his parents or the fact his father owned this entire resort.

He wasn't the man she thought he was. Not at all.

Stay out of this. It's a private matter. It doesn't concern you.

Gah. Why hadn't she done that? Enjoyed a nice weekend away. Stuck to her original plan. Kept her heart out of the equation. Now it was shattered on the floor, along with any hope of things continuing with Zac past this weekend, of them having more than a few nights of sex, being more to each other.

"Thank you, ladies," Ellen said. "Now for the announcement. After several rounds of interviews, and extensive face-to-face meetings this weekend, the candidate we've chosen for the job is…"

All Carmen wanted to do at that moment was to go back to her room and curl up in a ball to nurse her broken heart, to berate herself for being such an idiot. Whatever had made her think playboy Zac would settle down with *her*?

"Carmen Sanchez!" Ellen beamed down at her from the stage. "Congratulations, Carmen. We're so excited to welcome you to our California practice, and we're looking forward to all the amazing new protocols you'll put in place soon."

People rushed to congratulate her.

She responded in a fog.

Zac remained by her side, stiff as a stone, and his parents lingered as well.

Finally he leaned closer and said, "I'm going back to the room."

He started toward the side exit and his parents followed.

"We're not done here, son," his father called, racing after Zac with his wife in tow.

Carmen turned to Ellen and Liz. "If you'll excuse me? I need to check on my fiancé."

She hurried toward the exit and was almost to the door when the shaking started. Mild at first, like the vibrations of a large truck passing by on the road outside, gradually getting worse until the large chandelier at the center of the room swayed. A low, distant roar—like a freight train approaching—reached a crescendo and the world shook.

Earthquake.

They were having an earthquake.

Not a bad one, given what she'd seen following the seven point zero magnitude one in Anchorage the year prior, but still enough to send dishes crashing off carts and pictures flying off the walls. People huddled together for safety, and some even crawled under the tables. Several older attendees had been knocked to the ground, but no one seemed badly injured, thank goodness.

Earthquakes weren't uncommon in Alaska, especially smaller ones, but even so, Carmen's heart rate tripled, and she braced herself in the exit doorway until the tremor stopped and the roar of the sound waves faded away.

Legs quaking, she fumbled her way out of the exit and into the hall, only to find Zac crouched beside an older man on the floor.

It was his father, with his wife kneeling beside him, weeping softly. "Please, Zac. Don't let your father die. Please!"

"I'll do the best I can, Mom. I swear."

"What happened?" Carmen stood amongst the crumbled plaster and shattered glass on the floor, her brain taking a moment to register it all. "Was it the earthquake?"

"No. I don't know." Zac was in full EMT mode, taking the man's pulse, then ripping open his shirt to start CPR. "Call 911, Carmen. Now!"

She fumbled her phone out of her purse and

did as he asked, before rushing over to his side. "ETA five minutes on the ambulance."

He didn't miss a beat in the CPR—a credit to his skill as a paramedic.

"Thank you for calling them."

"Of course," she said, kneeling and switching into nurse mode, taking over chest compressions while he gave his father life-saving breaths. "Even though it's a private matter and doesn't concern me."

At least he had the decency to look ashamed when she threw his earlier words back in his face.

"I'm sorry..."

The wail of sirens grew closer outside, matching the screeching hurt inside Carmen. He'd been clear about not wanting a commitment up front, but that was little comfort to her broken heart now. She'd fallen for Zac way too hard and way too fast, against all her wishes to the contrary.

She should've known better.

She should've done better.

Hurt almost overwhelmed her before she shoved it aside, behind a wall of professional necessity. Right now she had a patient to save. Her pain would wait until later.

Same as it always did.

CHAPTER ELEVEN

"WE'VE GOT HIM, SIR," the paramedic said as they loaded Zac's father into the back of an ambulance a short time later.

They'd had to use the defibrillator to restart his father's heart. He was breathing on his own now, though Zac knew only too well from experience how quickly a patient's status could change. His emotions were a mess—anxious, sad, pissed off and remorseful. All at the same time.

He couldn't help thinking that this was his fault, even though logically he knew that was ridiculous.

"We'll take him to the hospital in town, then I'm guessing he'll be airlifted to Anchorage as soon as he's stable."

"Thank you."

Zac helped his mother into the back of the ambulance. She looked so much smaller and more fragile than he remembered. She clung to his father's limp hand like a lifeline and Zac's troubled heart fractured a bit more. Whether he understood it or not, his mother loved his father, and she'd be devastated if anything happened to him.

"I'll come up as soon as I get things settled here at the hotel, Mom."

He stood back to let the EMTs shut the rear doors of the rig, then watched as they drove off, lights and sirens blaring in the cold, dark night. Just an hour prior he'd vowed to turn his back on his parents and never see them again. Now he was right back into the thick of it with them and he had no idea how he felt about it. It was like a case of emotional whiplash—hating his father one second, then fearing he'd lose the man forever the next.

Behind him, he felt the weight of Carmen's stare on him and knew he had another hard battle yet to fight. He'd not missed the look of shock on her face when he'd told her the truth about his parents, nor the way that shock had given way to betrayal. A feeling he was all too familiar with from his own past.

"Look, I'm sorry I didn't tell you sooner. I should have been truthful right up front." He turned slowly to see her huddled inside his tux jacket, her arms crossed beneath the expensive fabric and her green-gold eyes spitting fire at him. "I don't know what else to say except I'm sorry."

"You don't trust me." She looked anywhere but at him. "I get it. This whole weekend was about pretending. You played your part well. I guess I thought we were friends, but I shouldn't have expected that to change anything. I mean, like you said, it's not my concern. I'm not important enough for you to tell me the truth about your identity."

Not important enough?

He lowered his head to stare at his feet. Dirty icy slush covered his shiny black loafers, and if that wasn't a metaphor for this disaster of an evening then he didn't know what was.

"We are friends."

And I wanted us to be so much more...

Instead of saying those words, however, he bit them back out of old habit. "And you are important to me, Carmen. I wanted to tell you so many times over this weekend, but the timing was never right."

He cringed, his father's words from earlier ringing in his head.

People are fallible, son. We fall down. We make mistakes.

Well, Zac sure as hell had made his share of them where Carmen was concerned.

He scrambled to keep his head above water.

"If it helps, I've never told anyone in Anchorage about my true identity."

"It doesn't help."

Yeah, he hadn't thought it would. Worse, he deserved all the ire she could pour out on him after the way he'd deceived her. Deserved to lose her, same as his father had almost lost his mother, because he was no better than his old man.

A liar. A cheat. A fraud.

Just as he'd always feared.

Well, if things were going down the drain, he might as well get it all out there in the open.

"Look, at first I didn't tell you because I didn't trust you—though it's not just you... I don't trust anyone. But later I didn't tell you because I didn't want to ruin your big weekend. And I didn't want to lose what we had last night."

"I see."

The small crowd that had gathered in the parking lot after the earthquake were slowly making their way back inside now the building inspectors had deemed the structure safe.

Carmen moved closer to him, out of the line of traffic, her expression dark. "You didn't tell me so I'd keep sleeping with you?"

"No. That's not what I meant."

"Well, that's what you said."

She'd crossed her arms again and was tap, tap, tapping that toe of hers on the ground. Never a good sign.

"I always knew you were a player, but that's low even for you."

"We had an agreement. No strings. *Your* rules, not mine."

He hated bringing it up, but she had him on the defensive now, and with everything else going on he felt raw and vulnerable and way too exposed, so he lashed out.

"This whole fiasco wouldn't have even happened if you hadn't asked me here, Carmen, so don't go blaming me if things didn't turn out the way you wanted. I played my part. I acted like your doting fiancé. Based on how much you enjoyed yourself last night, I'd say you got your money's worth. Because that's all *I* was here for, right?"

Her face had paled beneath the overhead lights, but he was on a roll now.

"You don't see me as anything but your fake boy toy. Because you work too damned much and too damned hard to have time for a real relationship. All you do is sacrifice for others and never take anything for yourself. *Poor Carmen, martyring herself on the altar of everyone else's happiness and well-being.* I thought maybe a weekend away might show you the error of your thinking. But I was wrong. You're alone because you like being alone. So fine. *Be* alone. Enjoy."

"How dare you? I cared for you, Zac. Beyond friendship. Way beyond liking. I—" She stopped herself and cursed under her breath. "Fine. Whatever. As far as I remember, you enjoyed yourself as much as I did. Then again, you enjoy yourself with a lot of women. Like father like son, apparently. Who knew bed-hopping was genetic?"

Zac froze, fists clenched at his sides, livid. Her words had struck far too close for his comfort. *Dammit.* He didn't have time for this. He needed to come to terms with the fact that the entire universe he'd carefully constructed these last twelve years had crumbled at his feet. He needed to get away from Carmen before he said something else he'd regret forever.

He brushed past her, ignoring the pain in her eyes that slashed his heart into pieces. "Congratulations on your new job in California."

Tonight had been a huge mess, and now he needed to pick up the shattered pieces and get on with the rest of his life.

Or what was left of it.

Carmen went back to the suite in something of a daze, too numb to cry. This evening had not turned out like she'd planned. Not at all. She'd gotten the job of her dreams and had a bright future ahead of her—could take care of her mother and her sister as she'd always wanted. And yet it all felt hollow somehow.

Far too amped-up to sleep, despite the late hour, she began packing instead. That way when Zac returned he would see she was ready to put all this behind her and move on.

Once her bags were packed, and she'd showered and changed into her PJs, Carmen slumped down on the sofa in the living room and stared out the window at the approaching dawn. It was going on six a.m. now and there was no sign of Zac returning. Just as well, since she was in no mood to see him again at the moment anyway.

How dared he accuse her of playing the martyr, of overextending herself for selfish reasons? He knew nothing about her. Not really. He didn't know her struggles. She snorted and looked around at her lavish surroundings. Apparently *he'd* grown up in the lap of luxury.

Carmen closed her eyes and let her head fall back against the cushion. Images of the hallway after the earthquake haunted her—Zac performing CPR on his father while his mother wept at his side, the desperation on his handsome face. That hadn't been the look of a man at peace with his life. That had been the look of a man who'd made major mistakes and feared he'd never have a chance to atone.

She sighed and straightened again. Not her problem. Not her issue to deal with anymore. Like he'd said. Not her concern.

Zac Taylor was out of her life and she'd do just fine. Because she was a survivor. She didn't need Zac. She didn't need anyone.

She'd give her notice at Anchorage Mercy as soon as she got home, put their modest little house on the market, then move with her family to California and put all this ugliness behind her. She'd get her mother set up at a nice assisted-living facility. She'd get Clara enrolled in the university of her choice near Big Sur. She'd forget all about Zac and her pipe dream of the two of them having any sort of lasting relationship.

He was a player. Carmen should have known better. Going forward, Carmen would do better.

"What doh kill does fatten." What doesn't kill you makes you stronger.

Right.

Now, if she could just get her battered heart back with the program, she'd be all set.

CHAPTER TWELVE

A COUPLE OF days later Carmen was making dinner at home. She had a rare night off and hoped to make the most of it by starting to pack up some things around the house.

After returning from the conference she'd basically gone into "blinder" mode—focusing on all the tasks she needed to do to prepare for the upcoming move to California.

They'd arrived back at Ted Stevens Airport and she and Zac had gone their separate ways without another word to each other. Lance and Priya had both asked her if everything was all right and she'd explained the whole situation to them—including the fake engagement—figuring she had enough deception in her life to last her a lifetime.

Prior to leaving the resort she'd told Ellen and Liz that she and Zac had broken up. They'd felt badly for her, but had said it didn't change their decision to hire her for the new supervisor position. She was still their top choice for the job.

The truth was out there now—sort of. She and Zac weren't engaged anymore.

Funny, but she'd expected to feel better about that than she did.

For the past few days she'd kept her head down and her vision focused. She'd turned in her resignation at Anchorage Mercy, begun transitioning her current patients to other midwives on staff, and generally started the slow, sad process of pulling up her roots here in preparation for putting them down elsewhere.

And, yes, maybe in the wee small hours before dawn her mind might return to the weekend with Zac. To how blissful everything had been with him until it hadn't been anymore. To the way it had felt lying in his arms, holding him close, kissing him under the brilliant Northern Lights.

But she'd firmly remind herself that he'd lied to her about his true identity. That he probably would've continued to lie to her for the foreseeable future if he'd not gotten caught. After all, she'd been the wronged party. She'd been the one in the right.

Then images of Zac's gravely ill father would fill her head. So many times she'd started to pick up the phone to call, to ask him if he needed anything, but then she'd hung up. He'd walked away from her that night. He'd said he didn't need her, didn't want her in his life any longer. He wouldn't appreciate her intrusion now.

Ugh. She stirred the thick soup simmering on the stove and sighed. All of it was such a shame.

She'd heard through the grapevine at the hospital that Zac's father had been transferred to the Cardiac ICU after they'd returned. Rumor had it he was doing better, though stent surgery to open a couple of blocked arteries in his heart was going to be necessary. The procedure itself was a fairly routine operation these days, but that still wouldn't lessen the stress on his loved ones. Anytime a member of your family went under the knife it was hard.

Speaking of families, her mama was at the kitchen table now, supervising Carmen's cooking as usual. She might have early-onset dementia, but that didn't stop the woman from bossing her daughters around in the kitchen.

"What's wrong, girl?" Mama looked up from the magazine she was paging through, frowning. "Time longer dan twine."

"I know…" Carmen leaned a hip against the edge of the counter while she stirred. Mama was right. Even the worst problems came to an end, if given time. She just wished it would be sooner rather than later. "I've just got a lot going on right now."

"Hmm…" Her mother flipped another page. "Wouldn't have anything to do with dat man you went to the resort with, would it?"

"No." *Yes.* Mama had always been far too observant for her own good. "I'm busy, that's all. Trying to get ready for the move and all. Plus, work's been crazy, and I'm training my replacement. It's a lot."

"But are you happy?" Mama looked up at her, eyes clear and expression lucid. "Dis what you want?"

"Of course." Carmen turned away and got things together to set the table. "It's the perfect job at the perfect clinic. I've worked hard to get the position and I'll earn enough money so we won't have to worry anymore."

"Worry?" Clara asked, dropping her backpack in the corner as she came in, then grabbing the bowls from Carmen's hands to set the table. "What are you guys talking about?"

"I asked your sister if she was happy," Mama said. "Since she been mooning around like a lost puppy after her weekend away."

"You've noticed too, eh?" Clara looked back at Carmen over her shoulder.

That was the great thing about families— you could put on the bravest face you could and they still saw through your BS. That was also the worst thing about them. She'd never been good at fooling people, least of all her family.

Clara got silverware from the drawer beside the sink. "It's Zac, isn't it? You like him. I can tell. Is it serious?"

"No." *Yes. Ugh.* "It's not about him. Not really." Carmen turned off the burner under the soup and shook her head. "He lied to me. After what Papa did, I won't tolerate a man's lies."

Mama snorted. "Your father was a rogue and a rebel, but he never lied."

Carmen filled each of the bowls with soup, then put the pot back on the stove. "Yes, he did, Mama. He walked out on us, remember?" She took a seat at the table beside her sister and across from their mother. "He never told you about his family and fortune back in Buenos Aires. Just left us behind the first chance he got."

"That's not true. I knew who and what he was from the start." Mama blew on a spoonful of steaming hot soup before eating it. "There was no deception."

The two sisters exchanged a glance. This was new information.

Carmen sipped her soup, a savory, thick mix of split peas, corn, chicken broth, potatoes, carrots, celery, thyme and pimento peppers. It was a taste of home that always made her miss the island. "Mama, I think you're mistaken. Papa—"

"No, child. I'm not mistaken." Mama fixed her girls with a serious stare. "My mind might be going sometimes these days, but I still know what's true. I remember talking to your daddy the first night we met. Remember it as clear as day. He told me plain about his obligations to his family's business and that he might have to go home someday. But we were in love and it was a chance I was willing to take. Besides, he gave me you two beautiful girls, so I can't complain."

"He *left* us," Clara said, scowling. "What kind of man walks out on his children?"

"The kind that's told to."

"His wealthy family put pressure on him?" asked Carmen, nibbling on a hunk of corn from her soup.

"No. I insisted he leave." Mama scowled. "His father had died and it was his duty to take over the company. Your papa was torn. The fact he had two different lives was eating him up inside. I loved him too much to let that happen. So I told him I didn't need half a man. Told him to go home. Told him to take his money too. He wanted to stay, wanted to put us up in a fancy house and send money every month, but I didn't want it. Looking back, I suppose I should have taken it. But I loved my life and my independence too much."

Carmen blinked at her mother a moment. "Wait. So you're saying Papa wanted to take care of us, but you refused?"

"Yes. I thought I could do it all on my own. Stand on my own two feet. I don't regret my choices, but I can see now that I deprived you girls of the opportunity to know your father and to know the truth." Mama sighed and shook her head. "Carmen, I'm telling you this because if you care for this man perhaps you should forgive him, give him a chance to make amends. If you truly want him, don't make the same mistakes I did. You can have love and a life too."

"But Papa never tried to contact us," Clara said. "He just walked away."

"No." Mama's expression turned sad. "He kept his distance out of respect for my wishes. I hurt him badly by cutting him out of our lives. Now it's too late. He died a few years ago, during a climbing accident in the Andes. I'm sorry, girls. I never meant to hide this from you for so long. But time's short and you deserve to know."

The sight of their mother's tears had Carmen and Clara out of their seats and around the table to comfort her. The woman might have made mistakes, but she was still the strongest person Carmen had ever known.

"It's okay, Mama," Carmen said, resting her head against her mother's shoulder. "Seems this is a time for coming clean all around."

"Yeah." Clara sniffled. "Me too. I…uh…got word this afternoon that one of the scholarships I applied for came through. So I can afford to stay here and go to nursing school in Anchorage. It covers tuition, books, room and board. Everything!"

"That's amazing!" Carmen hugged Clara, fresh tears stinging her eyes—happy ones this time. "I'm so happy for you."

"And I've decided I want to move into that nice assisted-living facility down the street," Mama said after they'd finished hugging and congratulating Clara. "The one with the pretty gardens in back."

Carmen sat back on her heels. "You just said you love your independence. Assisted living would mean giving that up."

"I know." She patted Carmen's hand and smiled. "But it's time. You go off to your fancy new job in California and be free. Beat de iron while it hot."

"But, Mama…" Her chest constricted. The whole reason she'd gone for the position at the clinic in Big Sur was to support her mother and her sister. Without that, was the extra money worth the pain of leaving behind the place she now called home?

"Sis…?" Clara reached over and took Carmen's hand. "That *is* what you want, right?"

She shook her head. "I don't know anymore. I thought it was, but now I'm not so sure. For so long I've been so busy moving ahead. I never considered things might be fine as they are."

"What about this man?" Mama asked.

"What about him?" She hadn't seen Zac since they'd parted at the airport, and after the way they'd left things there was little chance he'd want anything to do with her again. "I doubt we can mend our ties."

"You never know until you try." Mama cupped Carmen's cheek and smiled. "You are such a treasure. He'd be lucky to have you, if he's what you want. But make haste while de sun shine, girl. Good men don't wait long."

Zac stood outside his father's hospital room, hesitant about going in. He'd worked the night shift the evening before and done his best to keep busy, so he wouldn't have a chance to brood about this conversation.

Talking with his mother in the waiting room during his dad's procedure had helped him see things in a different light where his father was concerned, but that didn't mean the old hurts had completely healed. They needed to have a talk, and this one had been a long time in coming.

He nodded at one of the residents who walked by in the hall, then took a deep breath for courage. Time to plunge in.

Zac opened the door and walked in to find his father looking smaller and older than he remembered. IVs and a blood pressure cuff were attached to one of his arms, and EKG wires extended out from the electrodes on his chest. The white hospital gown stood in stark contrast to his dark skin, and there was a half-eaten bowl of gelatin on the table over his bed, along with his reading glasses and a nearly completed crossword puzzle.

His mother sat in the chair beside the bed, the clack of her knitting needles keeping time with the beeps of the heart monitor.

Both his parents looked up when he walked in, making Zac halt in his tracks.

"Son!" His mom set aside her yarn and got up to give him a hug. "Come in…come in. I was hoping you'd stop by. I need a break. I'm going to take a walk down to the cafeteria and get a snack. Be back soon."

As she passed by the bed, she gave his father a stern *get your business done* look.

The door closed behind her, leaving Zac and his father to stare at each other awkwardly.

"Hey," Zac said at last, resisting the urge to fidget inside his paramedic's uniform. He'd come straight after his shift and hadn't taken time to run home and change. "Uh... How are you feeling?"

His father gave a curt nod. "Better. Thanks to you."

"I didn't do your surgery." Zac took the seat his mother had vacated, since it was the only one in the room besides the bed. "Just handled CPR until the ambulance arrived."

"Stop, son. You saved my life that night at the resort, from what I've been told." His father clasped his hands over his stomach. "I wouldn't still be here without you, so thank you. I'm sure it wasn't an easy choice."

Zac winced. Yeah, given the fight they'd had just before the quake, he'd had that coming. "I'm a professional. There was no decision to make. I save lives. That's what I do."

Silence fell between them once more, until finally Zac couldn't take it anymore. He was here to make amends, one way or another. Time to get it done.

"Listen, Dad. I'm sorry."

"For what?" his father asked, looking surprised. "I'm the one who owes you an apology,

Zac. I let the bad feelings between us fester for all these years. I'm the one who's made the mistakes here, not you."

"But this…" He waved a hand toward his dad. "Your heart… I brought that on the other night."

"Don't flatter yourself. I've had high cholesterol for years. Been on medication for it. Not that you'd know, since you haven't seen me." His father sighed. "Again, my fault. Not yours. The earthquake didn't help either. All those people to keep safe. All those repairs to make."

Zac couldn't argue with that. "Mom and I talked yesterday while you had your procedure. She helped me understand some things I didn't before. I don't condone your affair, and nor will I forget it, but I have a better picture of how things are now. I thought you should know. I'm not saying we can go back to the way things were before your infidelity, but I'm different now too. I have a life and a career that I love here in Anchorage, and I'm proud of that. But… well, I wouldn't mind having you and Mom be a part of my life again. We could maybe give it a trial run…see how it goes."

"Hmm…" His dad nodded, his forehead creasing as he blinked hard. "I'd like that, son."

The last word shook slightly, as if he were holding back tears. And, oddly enough, Zac found himself battling a sting at the back of his own eyes.

"Good."

His father smiled at last, his eyes slightly watery. "I feared we'd never get to this place."

"Me too." Zac sat back in the chair, the knots of tension between his shoulder blades easing. "But I'm glad we did."

"Same."

His father scooted up in the bed slightly, setting off the heart monitor. A nurse rushed in to check, waving at Zac before she departed again.

"So, explain to me about this girl of yours," his father said.

Now it was Zac's turn to frown. "She's not my girl, remember? The whole thing was a fake. We haven't seen each other since we got back, and as far as I know she's been busy getting ready to move her life away from Alaska."

His father shook his head. "You serious about this girl?"

"Maybe..." Zac wasn't sure his newfound accord with his father extended that far yet. "Why?"

"If you like her, she must be special." His father reached over to pick up his glasses and crossword puzzle. "Where's she moving to?"

"Big Sur."

"Gorgeous place. Just opened a new hotel

in that area a few years ago. Been looking for someone to run it for me." His father went back to working on his puzzle. "What's a word that starts with *f* and ends in *s*? Eleven letters? The clue's 'absolution.'"

"I don't need a job, Dad. I have one. I'm a paramedic. A great one—best in Anchorage."

Some of the knots in his stomach returned. Prior to their falling out, his father had expected Zac to follow in his footsteps. He hoped they wouldn't go right back to that again.

"I'm happy here," he said.

"Good." His father looked up at him then, his expression sincere. "That's all I ever wanted for you, son. To be happy. And if living here and saving lives is what does that for you, then I'm happy too. Truly. I just thought if you ever needed a place to stay when you came to visit your girl you'd have one at my place."

"And who says I'll be going to visit Carmen?" he asked, rolling his stiff neck.

Honestly, he would do more than visit her if she forgave him, but that was neither here nor there at the moment, until he talked to her and begged her forgiveness.

Zac sat up and blinked at his father. "That's it!"

"What?" His dad scowled.

"The answer." Zac pushed to his feet and

grinned. "Eleven letters. Starts with *f* and ends in *s*. Forgiveness. Clue absolution. I need to go."

"Thanks, son!" his father shouted as Zac ran out of the room. "Now, go get that girl of yours."

CHAPTER THIRTEEN

CARMEN WAS AT work the next evening, catching up on her documentation from the last two deliveries she'd done. With spring right around the corner, it seemed everyone was going into labor these days.

Speaking of labor, there was a certain phone call she'd been putting off that she needed to make...

"Hey." Priya came up beside her at the counter. "How are you doing?"

"Fine." And perhaps if she kept repeating that word one day it would be true. Carmen glanced sideways at her friend, glad to see her color had improved. "And you?"

"Okay." Priya leaned an elbow on the counter. "Getting ready for the big move?"

Carmen exhaled slowly. She'd not shared her decision with anyone else yet, but now was the moment. The moment she admitted she wanted to try and repair things with Zac and see if he wanted to try having a real relationship. The moment when she declared to the world that the future she wanted for herself was right here in Anchorage.

"I've decided to decline the job in Big Sur."

"What?" Priya took her by the arm and led her into the nearby staff lounge, shutting the door before continuing. "*Why?* That's been our whole focus for months."

"I know, but things have changed." Carmen sank down onto the sofa against the wall and toyed with the hem of her lavender scrub shirt. "My heart's just not in it anymore."

"Does this have anything to do with a certain hot paramedic in the ER who pretended to be your fiancé?"

"No. I mean, yes. I mean..." She shook her head, sending her curls bouncing around her face. "Zac's definitely part of it, but he's not the whole reason."

"But you guys are still into each other, right?" Priya took a seat on the other end of the sofa, facing her. "I mean, I'll admit I was suspicious at first, but then I saw you guys dancing and there was no denying the chemistry. I felt like *I* needed to get a room afterward."

Carmen chuckled. "We did like each other. A lot. But we made mistakes."

"I'm sorry." Priya patted her on the arm.

"Relationships are tough. Even fake ones. But what's the rest of the reason you're not taking the new job?"

"I'm happy *here*." She shrugged. "I love Anchorage Mercy and you guys and my patients. I don't want to give all this up and start over again from scratch."

"Makes sense." Priya twirled a piece of her long dark hair around her finger. "What about the money, though?"

"I make plenty here, and after talking with my mother and my sister the other night I found circumstances have changed. Some things are more important than money, you know?"

"I do know." Priya placed her hand on her stomach. "You're sticking around, then?"

"I am. I still need to call Ellen, though, and let her know. And I'm going to recommend you as my replacement." Carmen smiled.

"Oh, don't do that."

"Don't recommend you? Why?"

"My circumstances have changed as well." Priya grinned and patted her tummy. "Lance and I are expecting our first baby in December."

"Oh, my gosh!" Carmen hugged her friend tight. "That's fantastic. I'm so happy for you both! It also explains why you looked a bit green at the conference."

"Right?" Priya yawned. "Between all the naps

and the morning sickness it's been a challenge. Anyway, we've decided to stick close to Anchorage too. My parents are in Sitka, and his are in Vancouver, so not that far away. Plus, we've picked out a plot of land and we're talking to the builders next week about constructing our new house."

"How wonderful!"

Carmen sighed. She really was happy for her friend. Happy for Lance too. And for her mama and Clara. Everyone seemed to have found their place in the world. Her as well, even if that place would be a bit lonelier without Zac to share it. Still, she'd gotten this far in life on her own—she could keep going.

"I'm so thrilled for you both. Really."

"Thanks." Priya narrowed her gaze. "Will you be my midwife?"

Touched beyond words, Carmen nodded. "Yes! Of course!"

"Good." Priya took her hand. "Now for some advice. Don't give up on him."

"Who?"

"Zac. Lance says he's going through some stuff right now with his parents. Who knew the guy's family was loaded, huh? He never acted like that around any of us."

"No, he didn't…"

He'd never seemed anything but real with

Carmen, even when they'd been pretending to be engaged. Yes, he'd hurt her by not telling her the truth about his family and his background, but then considering the stories of his father's infidelity and Zac's estrangement from him because of it, she couldn't say she blamed him. Plus, given the conversation she'd had with her mother about her own papa and the falsehoods she'd believed about him growing up, it seemed they both had their share of daddy issues to deal with.

"He's a good man."

She closed her eyes and pictured Zac that first day at the airport, so handsome in his tweed blazer. Then later at the welcome reception in his tux, all suave and debonair. Then at the animal reserve, rugged in jeans and a T-shirt, kissing her under the stars. The bowling alley. The night they'd slept together. His scent, his taste, his voice…

God, she missed him so, so much.

Yearning squeezed at her chest before she pushed it aside.

Beat de iron while it hot…

Her mama's words echoed in her head. She was right. Carmen needed to stop wasting time and make use of the opportunities she had *now*. With her mother going into assisted living and her sister living in the dorms at college, for the first time in forever Carmen would have no one to look out for except herself. She could go where she wanted, do what she wanted, be whoever she wanted. She should stop being scared about it and instead embrace her freedom.

But first she had a phone call to make.

She pushed to her feet and walked over to the phone on the wall. "I need to call Ellen."

"Right. And I need to go check on my patients." Priya started out the door, then leaned back into the room to give her a thumbs-up. "You got this, girl."

"Thanks."

Carmen waited until she was alone to dial the number, swallowing hard as it connected.

"Big Sur Women's Health Clinic," said a receptionist in a bright tone. "How may I direct your call?"

"Ellen Landon, please. Tell her it's Carmen Sanchez calling."

"Certainly. One moment, please, Ms. Sanchez."

Generic instrumental music played in the background before Ellen picked up.

"Carmen! Great to hear from you. How are preparations going for the move? Liz and I were just talking about you last night. I planned to call you later in the week to invite you down to stay with us for the weekend. Thought we could show you around Big Sur and help you get acclimated before the big move."

"Oh, that's very sweet," said Carmen, digging the toe of her white running shoe into the tile floor. "But I'm afraid I've got some bad news. I won't be accepting the position after all."

There was a slight pause, and Carmen lived and died in those few seconds.

"I'm so disappointed to hear that, Carmen," Ellen said. "Can you tell me what changed your mind? At the conference you seemed so interested in the job."

"I was. It's a great opportunity. But after a lot of thought and introspection I've come to realize I'm happy here and I want to stay in Anchorage."

"This doesn't have anything to do with your friend Zac, does it?" Ellen asked.

"No. Not really," Carmen said. "I actually haven't even seen him since we got back home. My circumstances here have changed, though, and I've decided to go in a different direction for my future."

"I'm sorry to hear that for us, but I wish you the best of luck." Ellen sighed. "Well, I guess I need to get a hold of Ms. Shaw, then."

Carmen wanted to tell her not to, but then figured it was Priya's news to tell. "I do want to thank you again for the opportunity, Ellen. It was such an honor to meet you and I hope we can stay in touch. You never know what might change down the road."

"Absolutely." Ellen's warm smile was palpable through her tone. "It was a pleasure meeting you too, Carmen. Finding such caring and dedication is rare these days and much appreciated. I'll keep in touch."

Once the call had ended, Carmen went back down to the ER just in time for a new case.

"Anchorage Mercy, this is FA18. Stand by for arrival of suspected placental abruption. Twenty-five-year-old patient in labor, thirty-nine weeks' gestation. Bleeding vaginally. Over."

Carmen rushed to slip into a clean gown and gloves, and was ready by the ER bay doors as the ambulance pulled up. The mother was full-term, but there were any number of problems that could develop if the placenta detached before the baby was born—including death. Tom Farber, the OB on call that night, stood beside her, ready and waiting in case the worst happened.

Within seconds the automatic doors whooshed open and the EMTs raced inside with a woman on a gurney, her harried husband beside her. Carmen quickly scanned the team, but there was no sign of Zac. Even under these circumstances her heart still ached for him.

She forced the errant thoughts from her head as they wheeled the patient into Trauma Bay One. Susan, Zac's usual partner, gave her the rundown.

Carmen waited until they'd transferred the woman to the hospital bed, then moved in beside her. "Hello, my dear. My name's Carmen Sanchez. I'm the midwife on duty in the ER tonight. Can you tell me if this is your first pregnancy?"

"No." The woman's breath caught on a sob. "My third. My daughter's five and I had another baby, but it was stillborn last year. Please save my baby. *Please.*" She cried out as another contraction hit hard.

Carmen looked down to see Tom performing the pelvic exam.

"Fresh red blood," he said. "Right. Let's get Mom hooked up to the heart monitors and see how Baby's doing."

Fresh blood wasn't good. Not good at all.

The woman clung to Carmen's arm. "Please, no surgery."

"She's terrified after her sister had a bad experience," the husband said. "She hates hospitals all around, actually. That's why we were trying to have the baby at home."

"Without any help?" Carmen gave him a side-glance. "With her history, that's very risky."

"I just wanted to make her happy," the husband said, clearly distraught. "Don't let her die, please. Save her and the baby. *Please.*"

"We'll do our best," Tom said, motioning with his head for one of the nurses to get the husband out of there. "Now, Ms.…?"

"Woznichak," Susan supplied helpfully.

"Right. What's your first name, hon?" Carmen asked, holding the woman's hand.

"Lonnie," she managed to say between panting breaths. "The baby's coming!"

"Yes, it is." Carmen gave the woman her best reassuring smile. "And we'll be here with you every step of the way."

"Okay," Tom said from the end of the table. "Fetal heart rate looks good, no distress as yet, so we're going to continue in the traditional way for now." He smiled at Lonnie, then checked the nearby monitor. "On the next contraction I want you to push as hard as you can, okay?"

Lonnie nodded and gave a primal growl, bearing down hard, her back arched.

"Yes!" Carmen said, happy to take the role of cheerleader. The patient's face had turned a mottled mix of red and purple with effort. "That's it, Lonnie. Very good!"

At last the contraction subsided, only to give

way to another. They were coming close together.

"Won't be long now," Carmen said, nodding to Tom.

"Nope. Almost there," he said. "I can see the head."

Lonnie screamed as another contraction hit, and gripped Carmen's hand so hard she thought her fingers might snap.

"Breathe!" Carmen said, coaching her through the pain. "That's it! That's it!"

"Head's out," Tom said. "One more push and you're done, Lonnie."

A squelching "pop" sounded and Lonnie went limp on the table, tears and sweat streaming from her face as she stared down at the newborn in Tom's hands. "Is that him?"

"Yes." He placed the baby on her chest before cutting the umbilical cord. "You have a gorgeous baby boy."

The father came around the curtain to kiss his wife and dote on his son and Carmen couldn't stop grinning. This was what she loved most about her job. Welcoming new life into the world.

After helping with the delivery of the placenta and the clean-up, Carmen felt tired but proud. She exited the trauma bay to see Susan at the nurses' station, clearly waiting for her.

Huh? That was odd. Usually the EMTs went back to their rigs after a call.

She discarded her soiled things into the biohazard bin, then washed up in the sink in the hall. Once she'd dried her hands, she walked back to where the other woman was standing. Her first thought was to ask how Zac was doing, but she didn't want to come off as unprofessional.

"Hey," she said, feigning interest in the calendar on the wall. "How are you, Susan?"

"Okay," the EMT said. "But I'll be better if you can help my partner out."

"Huh?" Carmen glanced over her shoulder, frowning, only to stop short at the sight of Zac, standing there in the ER in his tux—the same one from the conference—looking just as handsome as she remembered.

Susan grinned. "Seems Zac, here, lost his heart a few days back, and he thinks you're the only one who can help him find it again."

"I got it from here, Susan—thanks," said Zac. Then he stepped forward and dropped to one knee in front of Carmen. "I know I screwed up, big-time. And I know I have no reason to expect you to trust me ever again. I know I lost the best thing that ever happened to me when I let you go, Carmen Sanchez, but if you can find it in your heart to forgive me, I swear I'll spend the rest of my life making it up to you."

Stunned, Carmen stared down at him, trying to take it all in. People were starting to stare, and heat crept up her cheeks. "Zac, get up. What are you doing?"

"I'm bowing before my queen." He looked up at her and winked. "Can you forgive me?"

She sighed and shook her head, laughing. "There's nothing to forgive, Zac. I'm as much to blame for what happened at the resort as you. It was my plan in the first place."

"But I went along with it. And I lied to you about who I really was."

He glanced around at the small crowd of staff who'd gathered. Word had spread like wildfire about his wealthy background once they'd gotten back to Anchorage Mercy. He knew Carmen had never said a word, but somehow the hospital rumor mill knew all.

"I should've been honest with you from the start, but back then I couldn't even be honest with myself."

"I wasn't exactly winning any awards in the honesty department myself," she said, then gestured toward a small empty supply room nearby. "How about we get some privacy?"

He nodded and followed her into the tiny

room. The overhead fluorescent lights flickered on automatically, sensing their presence.

"So…" he said, his hands in his pockets and his gaze focused on his toes.

"So."

This close to him she could feel his heat through her thin scrubs and smell his cologne. She'd missed both those things more than she could say. Missed everything about him, really.

"I guess you've been busy packing for California?" he said at last.

"Actually, I turned down the job." She huffed out a breath. "I decided everything I wanted was already here in Anchorage."

Zac did look up then. "You did?"

"I did. Called Ellen earlier to tell her. I was going to recommend Priya take my place, but then…" She stopped before spilling her friend's secret, in case Zac didn't know.

"Yeah. Lance is over the moon about the baby. It's all he talks about anymore. 'My son this' or 'my daughter that.'" He grinned. "Not that I blame him. Hope to have a couple of my own someday."

"Me too." She pursed her lips and rocked back on her heels. "Look, Zac. I'm sorry too—about the things I said to you. How you choose to live your life is none of my business. I'm afraid I let my old biases affect my life now, and for that you have my apologies. I talked with my mom after I got back, and she straightened me out on a few things."

"Like what?"

"Like the fact that my dad did want to take care of us, but she chose to refuse his help because she was stubborn and wanted to do things on her own."

"I see." He bit back a smile. "Sounds like someone else I know."

"Do you want to hear my apology or not?" she asked, needing to get it all out before she couldn't. "I shouldn't have judged you for your past any more than I would want you to judge me for mine. Neither of us had any control over what happened back then."

"Agreed."

"But I do think it might be good for you to at least talk to your father and try to reconcile. Family is one of the most important things there is in this world, Zac. It's not healthy to be alone. Especially with your father's illness. If he died and you'd never made amends that would haunt you for the rest of your days."

"Also agreed. My father's doing fine, by the way. He's had three stents put in and is being released from hospital today," Zac said. "And we did talk. My mom too. It's all good. Well, as good as can be expected for now. They're heading back to the resort."

"Wow. Okay, then…" She had to admit she was impressed. Zac was a take-charge kind of man. Another one of the things she loved most about him. "That's great."

"Know what else is great?" he asked, inching closer to her.

She shook her head, not trusting her voice as her pulse notched higher.

"The fact that for the first time in over a decade I'm finally free. Free of the guilt and the secrets and the shadow of betrayal. I feel like a new man."

"Yeah?" she squeaked.

There was only about an inch separating them now. Still, Carmen stood her ground, not willing to give up this time for anything in the world.

"Yeah. And as a new man I'm looking to settle down with the right woman."

Swallowing hard, she could only nod up at him.

"I want you to be that woman, Carmen, if you'll have me. If you can find it in your heart to forgive me and grant me another chance." He reached up slowly to take her chin between his thumb and forefinger. "I promise that if you do I will spend the rest of my life treating you like the precious treasure you are. *Can* you forgive me, Carmen?"

Mouth dry and head spinning, she gave him a trembling smile. "Yes, Zac. Yes!"

Next thing she knew she was in his arms and he was kissing her deeply—and, man, oh, man, she hadn't realized how badly she wanted this until she felt his firm lips on hers.

When he pulled away at last, they were both breathless.

"I love you, Carmen Sanchez," he said, his forehead resting against hers.

"I love you too, Zac Taylor," she said. Then she pulled back to look up at him through her lashes and give him a mischievous grin. "Although I do have one condition."

"What's that, darling?" He clasped his hands behind her lower back.

"That you take me back to that resort of yours someday and treat me to all the amenities I missed out on the first time."

"Count on it, my queen." He laughed and lifted her into his arms. "Your wish is my command."

CHAPTER FOURTEEN

One year later...

THE WEDDING DAY was gorgeous. Sunshine, blue skies and all their friends and family gathered in the gardens behind Anchorage Mercy Hospital. Considering it was where he and Carmen had first met, it seemed only right that it was where Zac and the woman he loved should start their life together as man and wife.

After they'd made their vows and sealed it with a kiss, the entire party flew over to the Arctic Star Resort for the reception. Zac's father had paid to have the whole gang flown there.

Jake and Molly and their twins. Tom and Wendy and their new baby, and Tom's daughter Sam. Carmen's mother. Even Zac's parents and Dustin. Priya was there too, with her adorable baby girl, Kaia. Lance had been his best man, of course, and Carmen's sister Clara her maid of honor.

The whole day couldn't have gone any better, and now there wasn't a dry eye in the house as Zac led his beautiful bride out onto the dance floor for their first dance. He nodded to the DJ and Michael Bublé crooned the lyrics to "The Way You Look Tonight," the song they'd danced to that first night at the conference—the night they'd both started falling in love.

"Happy, darling?" Zac whispered near Carmen's ear as they swayed gently to the music.

"So happy," she said, beaming up at him. "Though I do have something to tell you."

His pulse stuttered a bit. After all the secrets and lies they'd overcome because of his past, he wasn't sure how many more surprises he could take.

"What? If it's another horrible secret, I may jump off O'Malley's Peak."

"No, silly." She shook her head. "This is a good secret. Well, I hope it will be good."

Zac swallowed hard. "Just tell me."

"I'm pregnant," she said, her green-gold eyes shining with happiness. "I know it's earlier than we planned, but these things happen sometimes, and—"

"You're having a baby?" Zac said, cutting her off.

He blinked down at her, trying to take it in. He'd always wanted a kid of his own, but had been scared he might not be a good father. A year ago he wouldn't have been ready. But now, after putting the past to rest and forgiving his father and himself, he was beyond excited.

"We're having a baby?"

She nodded, fresh tears sparkling in her eyes. "Are you happy?"

"Yes! I'm going to be a father!"

His grin grew by the second, and then carefully he picked Carmen up and spun her around in his arms while the crowd clapped.

"We're going to be parents!"

"Yes, we are!" Carmen hugged him tight. "I love you so much, *doux-doux*."

"And I love you too, darling," Zac said, kissing her sweetly.

* * * * *

If you enjoyed this story, check out these other great reads from Traci Douglass

A Mistletoe Kiss for the Single Dad
Finding Her Forever Family
One Night with the Army Doc

All available now!